THE INVINCIBLE

Stanisław Lem Titles from the MIT Press

Highcastle: A Remembrance, translated by Michael Kandel

His Master's Voice, translated by Michael Kandel

Hospital of the Transfiguration, translated by William Brand

The Invincible, translated by Bill Johnston

Memoirs of a Space Traveler: Further Reminiscences of Ijon Tichy,
translated by Joel Stern, Maria Swiecicka-Ziemianek, and Antonia Lloyd-Jones

Return from the Stars, translated by Barbara Marszal and Frank Simpson

THE INVINCIBLE

STANISŁAW LEM

translated by Bill Johnston

THE MIT PRESS
CAMBRIDGE, MASSACHUSETTS
LONDON, ENGLAND

This book was set in Dante Pro and PF Din by Jen Jackowitz. Design by Marge Encomienda. Printed and bound in the United States of America.

Library of Congress Cataloging-in-Publication Data

Names: Lem, Stanisław, author. | Johnston, Bill, 1960– translator.
Title: The invincible / Stanisław Lem ; translated by Bill Johnston.
Other titles: Niezwyciężony. English
Description: Cambridge, Massachusetts ; London, England : The MIT Press, [2020]
Identifiers: LCCN 2019024834 | ISBN 9780262538473 (paperback) | ISBN 9780262357678 (ebook) | ISBN 9780262357685 (ebook)
Classification: LCC PG7158.L39 N5413 2020 | DDC 891.8/5373—dc23
LC record available at https://lccn.loc.gov/2019024834

10   9   8   7   6

No one's conscious intentions, no hostile thought stood in our path.

CONTENTS

Science fiction has famously predicted many of the important technologies of the twentieth century: space travel, satellites, the atomic bomb, television, the internet, and virtual reality, to name a few. In *The Invincible*, Stanisław Lem predicts another: artificial life. Although speculations about self-reproducing artificial systems date from the 1940s, the scientific field received its name from Christopher Langton only in 1986, more than two decades after *The Invincible*'s original publication (1964). One of the central controversies in artificial life is whether evolutionary programs and devices are actually alive (the strong version), or whether they merely simulate life (the weak version). Researchers who follow the strong version argue that the processes embedded in software programs such as genetic algorithms are as "natural" as life itself; what is artificial is the medium in which these processes take place.

The issue prompted Robert Rosen, among others, to speculate about the essential characteristics of "life itself," not only as it evolved on Earth in carbon-based life forms but also about the possibility of life-as-it-could-be in exoplanetary systems, arguing that silicon-based artificial life forms may provide insight into these theoretical speculations.

The Invincible presents a fascinating hybridization of these different views. Dr. Lauda's hypothesis proposes that a space ship from the Lycran system landed on Regis III millions of years ago; while the biological visitors perished, the automata did not. There then followed an evolutionary struggle between the automata and the planet's indigenous life forms, on the one hand, and between the different kinds of automata, on the other. Such a scenario requires that the "survive and reproduce" mandate that governs life on Earth could also operate on this planet. Lem minimally fulfills the requirement by postulating that the automata could manufacture themselves with modifications dictated by evolutionary processes. Clearly his interest is not in filling out how this might take place (John von Neumann, encountering a similar problem, imagined metal parts floating on a lake that could self-assemble). Rather, Lem's focus is on envisioning an artificial life form that won the evolutionary competition on Regis III for profoundly different reasons than did *Homo sapiens* on Earth.

The effect is achieved by introducing a significant factor that has a monumental impact on evolutionary trajectories: rather than fulfilling their energy needs through ingesting food, the automata on Regis III evolve to use solar power. The smaller the artificial organism, the less energy it needs. Hence the evolutionary driver is toward smaller forms, which overcome not through superior intellect but through swarm intelligence. Lem added to this the ability of the swarm of "flies" to generate immensely powerful electromagnetic fields, which meant that the tiny automata are not only the evolutionary winners on their planet but a powerful force against the invading humans. Their tiny size notwithstanding, their awesome potential illuminates the profound ambiguity of the work's title, which can be taken to refer either to the spaceship's proud name or to the swarms of alien automata that threaten it.

Contemporary research in artificial life has validated Lem's insight that swarms of artificial beings require only a few simple rules to manifest complex behaviors and hence each member needs to carry only a little cognitive power onboard. Computer simulations that have accurately depicted swarm behaviors in fish, birds, bees, and other biota demonstrate that each individual responds only to the four or five closest to it, with rule sets that take up only a few lines of code. For example, a school of fish swimming to evade a predator is guided by the fish closest to the predator. The direction this most imperiled individual follows determines how the entire school will run as it flashes back and forth, a simple strategy that makes excellent sense, since the fish that has the most to lose will try hardest to escape. Although each fish's behaviors are simple, the collective result nevertheless generates swarm intelligence of considerable complexity.

Decades before these ideas became disseminated within the scientific community, Lem intuited that different environmental constraints might lead to radically different evolutionary results in automata compared to biological life forms. Although on Earth the most intelligent species (i.e., humans) has tended to fare the best, their superior intelligence comes with considerable costs: a long period of maturation; a lot of resources invested in each individual; socialization patterns that emphasize pair bonding and community support; and a premium on individual achievement. But these are not cosmic universals, and different planetary histories might result in the triumph of very different kinds of qualities.

The contrasts between humans and the automata swarm are brought out most poignantly in the scene between Captain Horpach and First Officer Rohan, in which the captain delegates to Rohan the decision whether to put another crew member in grave danger to determine if the missing four men have indeed perished, as seems all but certain, or whether one or more might still be alive. The assumptions that make this gamble even remotely worth taking are revealing: human life is precious; human solidarity depends on the crew's belief that everything possible will be done to save them if they are in peril; and every human is unique and therefore uniquely valuable. None of these, of course, holds true for the swarm, whose individual members are virtually identical to one another, with each tiny automaton easily replaced and therefore disposable. Consequently, none is valuable in itself; only the swarm has evolutionary survival value. The contest, then, is not only between different life forms but also between the different values that have resulted from the divergent evolutionary pathways of humans on Earth and the "flies" on this strange planet. As with *Solaris*, Lem suggests that assumptions born and bred of Earth may appear hopelessly provincial in light of human encounters with radically different life forms. From a broader cosmic perspective, the best of human science, engineering, and weaponry may reveal humans to be completely out of our depth, mere kindergarteners bidding for a place in the universe's adult civilizations. The reduction of crew members to infancy when attacked by the "flies" may be a metaphor for this realization.

Of all the human characters, Rohan has the strongest claim to have encountered the planet on its own terms. He has traversed its terrain with his own feet; he has mixed his sweat with its crevices, valleys, and hills; he has breathed its native atmosphere into his lungs. The insight he gains from his heroic trek therefore commands our respect. When he concludes that "not everything everywhere is for us [humans]," we are right to hear in this pronouncement Lem's own challenge to the anthropo-centric assumptions that continue to dominate human ethical frameworks as well as human exploitations of planet Earth. As with the best science fiction, *The Invincible* has as much to teach us about our present situations as any futures we may face.

N. Katherine Hayles
Distinguished Research Professor of English,
University of California, Los Angeles
June 2019

BLACK RAIN

———

The *Invincible*, a class II cruiser, the largest vessel of the fleet stationed at the base in the Lyra constellation, was moving in photon sequence across a quadrant on the very edge of that cluster of stars. The eighty-three men of the crew were sleeping in the tunnel-shaped hibernation chamber on the main deck. Since the journey was relatively short, rather than full hibernation they had been put into a deepened sleep in which body temperature did not drop below fifty degrees. Only automatons were working on the bridge. In the crosshairs of their field of vision was the disk of a sun that was not much hotter than a regular red dwarf. When it filled half the width of the screen the annihilation reactor was turned off. For some time, throughout the ship there was a dead silence. The air conditioning and digital instruments went on functioning without a sound. There was no longer the faint vibration accompanying the shaft of light that had previously been streaming from the stern and, like a sword of infinite length thrust into the darkness, had been propelling the ship forward. The *Invincible* continued to move at close to the speed of light: inert, mute, and seemingly deserted.

Then control lights began to wink at one another from the consoles bathed in the pink glow of the distant sun filling the main monitor. Ferromagnetic tapes started up, programs were slowly drawn in by one piece of equipment after another, the commutators gave off sparks, and current flowed into the cables with a hum unheard by anyone. The electric motors, overcoming the resistance of lubricating oil that had long gone unused, kicked into action, the sounds they made rising from a bass to a high-pitched whine. Lusterless cadmium rods slid out of the auxiliary reactors, magnetic pumps fed liquid sodium into the cooling coils, and a shudder passed through the metal flooring of the stern decks, while at the same time a faint pattering sound inside the walls, making them sound as if they were filled with entire herds of small animals tapping their claws against the metal, indicated that the moving automatic check-and-repair devices had already set off on their journey of many miles, inspecting every weld of the girders, testing the air-tightness of the hull and the integrity of the metal joints. The whole ship filled with murmurs and movement as it woke up; only its crew was still asleep.

Eventually, though, one of the automatons swallowed its program tape and sent a signal to the control center of the hibernation chamber. Waking gas mingled with the current of cool air. A warmth blew among the rows of bunks through the grilles in the floor. For a long time the crew seemed reluctant to wake up. Some moved their hands torpidly; their icy sleep, previously empty, was now being filled with nightmares and hallucinations. One of them finally opened his eyes. The ship was ready for it. A few moments earlier the long passageways of the decks, the elevator shafts, cabins, bridge, work stations and airlocks, till now plunged in darkness, had brightened with the white glare of artificial daylight. While the hibernation chamber swelled with a hum of human sighs and semiconscious groans, the ship, as if too impatient to wait for its crew to wake up, had begun the initial phases of deceleration. The main monitor showed streaks of fire from the nose. The stillness of sub-lightspeed travel was broken by a judder as the powerful prow-mounted rockets strove against the eighteen thousand tonnes of invariant mass of the *Invincible*, multiplied now by its immense velocity. In the cartography cabins the tightly stowed maps shook uneasily in their rolls. Here and there, objects that had not been fastened down shifted as if coming alive. In the galleys the dishes rattled; the backs of unoccupied foam arm-chairs were set rocking; and across the decks, the straps and cords along the walls started shaking. A clatter from the combined sounds of glass, sheet metal, and plastic passed through the entire craft from stem to stern. In the meantime, the sound of voices could already be heard from the hibernation chamber; after the nothingness they had been immersed in for seven months, the human beings there had passed through a short sleep and were now returning to a waking state.

3

The ship was reducing speed. The planet covered up the stars; it was swathed in wooly red clouds. The convex mirror of an ocean, in which the sun was reflected, moved past ever more slowly. A dull-colored continent dotted with craters hove into view. The men at their stations on the various decks saw nothing. Far below them, in the titanium-built innards of the engine room there was a growing roar; a powerful grav-itational pull prised hands from levers. The cloud cover that had come within reach of the rockets turned silver in a burst of mercury, scattered apart, and vanished. The boom of the engines intensified for a moment. The reddish disk flattened: The planet was turning into land. Windswept crescent-shaped dunes could be made out; fingers spreading like the spokes of a wheel from the nearest crater lit up with the reflected fire of the rocket's nose-cone, brighter than the light of the sun.

"Full axis power. Static thrust."

The needles eased lazily into the adjacent section of the scale. The maneuver went off without a hitch. The craft, like an inverted volcano breathing fire, was hovering half a mile above the pitted surface with its patches of rock half-buried in sand.

"Full axis power. Reduce static thrust."

It was already possible to see the place where the blast of the jet engines hit the ground vertically below. They kicked up a dark red storm of sand. Purple streaks of lightning shot from the stern, seemingly soundless as the noise they made was drowned out by the louder roar of the gases. The difference of potential evened out, the lightning faded. One bulkhead in the prow emitted a creak. The captain indicated it to the engineer with a nod of the head: resonance. That needed to be fixed. But no one said anything, the drive shafts wailed, and the ship descended, though now without a single shudder, like an iron mountain strung on invisible wires.

"Half axis power. Low static thrust."

Smoking waves of desert sand were blowing away in circles in every direction like breakers on an actual ocean. The epicenter, struck at close range by the unruly flame from the jets, was no longer giving off smoke. The sand had disappeared, turned into a mirror of blistered red, a seething lake of melted silica, a pile of loud explosions, till it evaporated. The ancient basalt of the planet, exposed like bone, began to soften.

"Atomic piles to neutral. Cold thrust."

The blue of the atomic fire faded. Diagonal streams of boranes burst from the nose cone jets and in a single moment the desert, the walls of the rocky craters, and the clouds above them were bathed in a spectral green. The basalt base on which the broad stern of the *Invincible* was to come to rest was no longer in danger of melting.

"Piles to zero. Cold thrust through landing."

Every heart was cheered; heads leaned over instruments; levers were gripped by sweaty palms. These time-honored words meant there was no turning back, that their feet would stand on real ground, even if it was only the sand of a desert globe; that there would be a sunrise and sunset, a horizon, and clouds, and wind.

5

"Landing point at nadir."

The *Invincible* was filled with the protracted howl of the turbines compressing the drive matter. A green, cone-shaped pillar of fire joined the ship to the steaming rock. Clouds of sand rose on all sides, obscuring the periscopes of the central decks; it was only on the bridge that the radar screens, fading in and out along with the circling signal, continued to show the outlines of a landscape plunged in typhoon-like chaos.

"Cut engines on contact."

Fire churned rebelliously under the stern, compressed by the vast body of the rocket inching down on top of it; the green inferno shot long tongues of flame deep into the quivering billows of sand. The gap between the stern and the scorched basalt was no more than a narrow crack, a green burning line.

"Zero and zero. Cut all engines."

A bell rang: a single chime, as if of a huge cracked heart. The rocket was still. The Chief Engineer stood with his hands on the two levers of the emergency jets, in case the rock subsided. They waited. The second hands of the clocks kept moving at their insect-like pace. The captain gazed for a while at the level indicator; its silvery light did not deviate in the slightest from the red zero mark. They were silent. The jet nozzles, which had gone cherry-red from the heat, began to contract, emitting a characteristic series of noises like hoarse grunts. The reddish cloud of sand, thrown hundreds of feet into the air, began to settle. The blunt top of the *Invincible* emerged out of it; then its sides, blackened by the atmospheric friction so it looked like ancient rock; then its double-plated hull. The red dust was still swirling around the stern, but the ship itself had come to a definitive standstill, as if it was now part of the planet and was turning along with its surface in a languid motion that had been going on for centuries beneath a purple sky in which the brightest stars remained visible, fading only in the immediate vicinity of the red sun.

"Regular procedure, sir?"

The star captain straightened up from the log book, where in the middle of the page he had written the customary symbol for landing, the time, and had added in the next column the name of the planet: Regis III.

"No, Mr. Rohan. We're going to start with degree three."

Rohan tried to mask his surprise.

"Yes, sir. Though," he added with a familiarity that Horpach often permitted him, "I'd rather not be the one to make the announcement."

As if he had not heard what his first officer had said, the captain took him by the arm and led him to the monitor as though to a window. The sand blown aside by the force of the landing had formed a kind of shallow basin ringed by crumbling dunes. From a height of eighteen floors they gazed, via a tri-colored surface of electronic impulses creating a faithful image of the outside world, at the jagged rock rim of the crater three miles away. To the west it receded beyond the horizon. To the east, impenetrable black shadows were gathering under its steep gullies. The broad rivers of lava, their tops rising above the sands, had the color of dried blood. One bright star burned in the sky near the upper edge of the screen. The upheaval brought about by the *Invincible*'s descent from the heavens had passed, and the desert wind, a fierce current of air blowing constantly from the equatorial regions toward the planet's pole, was already packing the first tongues of sand under the ship's stern, as if patiently seeking to heal the wounds caused by the fire from the jets. The captain turned on the exterior microphones and for a moment the high space of the bridge was filled with a virulent distant wailing along with the sound of sand scraping against the hull. He turned the microphones off again, and silence fell.

"That's how it looks," he said slowly. "But the *Condor* didn't return from here, Rohan." The latter's jaw tightened. He could not argue with his commander. They'd traveled many parsecs together, but had never become friends. Perhaps the age difference was too great. Or the dangers they had faced together too small. He was uncompromising, this man with hair almost as white as his uniform. Nearly a hundred men remained motionless at their stations after the intense labor that had preceded the approach: three hundred hours of deceleration of the kinetic energy amassed in every atom of the *Invincible*; entering into orbit; landing. Nearly a hundred men who for months had not heard the sound of the wind and had learned to hate the vacuum of space as only those who know it can. But that was certainly not what their commander was thinking about. He walked slowly across the bridge and, leaning a hand on a chair back that had been raised to a different height, murmured:

"We don't know what it is, Mr. Rohan."

Then suddenly, sharply:

"What are you waiting for?"

Rohan strode up to the control consoles, switched on the intercom and in a voice in which suppressed disapproval still trembled, said brusquely:

"Attention all decks! Landing complete. Degree three ground procedure. Eight deck: Prepare energobots. Nine deck: Activate shield batteries. Force field technicians to their stations. The rest of the crew, assume your positions. Over and out."

As he spoke, watching the green eye of the amplifier dance to the modulations of his voice, he imagined their sweat-bathed faces turning toward the speakers and freezing in sudden amazement and anger. It was only now they would understand, only now they'd begin to curse ...

"Degree three ground procedure underway, captain," he said without looking at the older man. Horpach glanced at him and unexpectedly smiled out of the corner of his eye.

"This is just the beginning, Mr. Rohan. Maybe later on there'll be long walks at sunset, who knows."

From a small wall cabinet he took out a tall slim volume, opened it and, placing it among the numerous levers on the white console, asked:

"Have you read this?"

"I have."

"Their last signal recorded by hyperrelay no. 7 reached the closest beacon to the base a year ago."

"I know what it said by heart. 'Landing on Regis III complete. Desert planet, sub-delta-92 category. Following degree two procedure; exiting onto land in the equatorial zone on the continent of Evana.'"

"Right. But that wasn't their last message."

"I know, sir. Forty hours later the hyperrelay recorded a series of impulses that appeared to be sent in Morse code but made no sense whatsoever; then some strange sounds that were repeated several times. Haertel described them as 'the mewling of cats being tugged by the tail.'"

"Right," said the captain, but it was clear he wasn't listening. He was standing in front of the monitor once again. At the very edge of the field of vision, right by the rocket, there had appeared the scissor-shaped struts of the ramp, down which, as if on parade, came an even line of energobots, thirty-ton machines plated with fireproof silicon. As they crawled along their shells gradually opened and rose upwards, increasing the space between them; leaving the ramp they sank deep into the sand, but they moved confidently, plowing through the dune that the wind had already formed around the *Invincible*. They dispersed alternately one way then the other, and within ten minutes the entire perimeter of the ship was marked by a ring of metal turtles. As each one came to a stop, it began to dig itself steadily into the sand till it vanished, and only shiny spots situated at regular intervals along the red slopes of the dunes indicated the places where turrets bearing Dirac transmitters poked out. The foam-covered steel floor of the bridge suddenly trembled underfoot. A distinct though barely perceptible shudder, brief as a flash of lightning, passed through the bodies of those present and was gone, though for a moment longer they felt a tingling sensation in their jaws, and their vision blurred. The whole thing lasted less than half a second. Silence returned, broken by the distant hum of the motors starting up in the depths of the ship. The desert, the black and red taluses, and the sluggishly moving waves of sand came into focus on the monitors and everything was as it had been before, but now the invisible dome of a protective force field extended over the *Invincible*. Down the ramp came metallic crabs, their rotating antennas moving now left, now right. These inforobots, much larger than the devices creating the force field, had flattened trunks and curving stilt-like legs extending from their sides. Plunging their legs into the sand and extracting them as if with disgust, the arthropods spread out and took up positions in the gaps between the energobots. As the shielding operation progressed, control lights flashed on beneath matted glass on the main console, and the disks of the percussion dials filled with a greenish glow. Now it was as if dozens of large cat's eyes were staring motionless at the two humans. All the needles rested at zero, indicating that nothing was attempting to pass through the invisible barrier of the force field. Only the power gauge climbed higher and higher, passing the red lines of successive gigawatt readings.

"I'm going to go down and get something to eat. Oversee the standard procedure, Mr. Rohan," said Horpach, his voice tired all of a sudden, as he stepped reluctantly away from the screen.

"Remotely?"

"If you'd rather, you can send someone. Or go yourself."

With these words the star captain slid open the door and left. For a moment longer Rohan could still see his profile by the faint light of the elevator, which moved noiselessly downward. He glanced at the force field indicators. Zero. Actually it would have been best to start with photogrammetry, he thought to himself. Orbit the planet long enough to gather a complete set of pictures. Maybe that way they would find something. Because visual observation from orbit was of little value; continents are not the sea, nor are observers with their telescopes sailors in the crow's nest, however many of them there are. It was another matter that acquiring a full set of photographs would have taken almost a month.

The elevator returned. He got in and rode down to six deck. The large platform in front of the airlock was crowded with people who in fact had nothing more to do there, all the more so since the four bells signaling the time for the main meal had been repeating for perhaps the last fifteen minutes. The men stepped out of his way.

"Jordan and Blank, you'll go set up the procedure with me."

"Full space suits, sir?"

"No, just oxygen masks. And one robot. Preferably one of the arctans, so it doesn't get stuck in this damn sand. The rest of you, what are standing around for? Have you lost your appetite?"

"We were hoping to go ... outside, sir."

"Just for a few minutes ..."

A buzz of voices arose.

"Easy, guys. There'll be time for outings. For the moment we have degree three." They grudgingly dispersed. In the meantime, a crane emerged from the service elevator carrying a robot that was a head higher than the tallest humans. Jordan and Blank, already wearing oxygen equipment, were returning in an electric cart—he watched them as he leaned against the handrail in a passageway that, now the ship stood on its stern, had turned into a vertical shaft running all the way down to the first machine bulkhead. Beneath and above him he was conscious of the multiple levels of the metal infrastructure; at the very bottom the quiet-running conveyors were operating, he could hear the faint slap of the hydraulic ducts, while from the depths of the hundred-and-thirty foot long shaft came the steady flow of cool purified air from the A/C unit in the engine room.

The two men working the airlock opened the door for them. Rohan automatically checked the placement of the straps and the tightness of his mask. Jordan and Blank followed him in, after which the metal plate creaked loudly from the steps of the robot. There was a fearful prolonged hiss of air being sucked into the interior of the ship. The external hatch opened. The machine ramp was four floors below. For the crew there was a small elevator that had already been extended from the hull. Its framework reached all the way down to the top of the dune. The cage was open on all sides. The air was not much cooler than on board the *Invincible*. The four men climbed in; the magnets were released, and the elevator moved smoothly down eleven floors, passing successive sections of the hull. Without thinking, Rohan checked their condition. Outside of the dock, opportunities to examine the ship from the outside were rare. It's been through a lot, he thought to himself, seeing the traces left by meteors. In places the armor plating had lost its sheen, as if it had been eaten away by a powerful acid. The elevator reached the end of its short run, coming to a gentle stop on a crest of windblown sand. The men jumped out and immediately sank in up to their knees. Only the robot, which had been designed to work in deep snow, moved in a comical, ducklike, but confident manner on its disproportionately large flat feet. Rohan ordered it to stop, while he and the other humans carefully examined all the outlets of the stern-mounted jets, to the extent that they were accessible from outside.

"They could use a clean and a polish," he said. It was only when he came out from under the stern that he noticed what a huge shadow the ship cast. It stretched like a broad roadway across dunes that were lit up by the already low sun. There was a particular calm in the regularity of the waves of sand. At their base they were filled with light blue shadows, while their tops were pink from the sunset, a warm, delicate tint that reminded him of colors he'd seen once in a children's picture book. It was so mild, in such an unreal way. He looked slowly from dune to dune, finding ever new shades of the peachy glow; the further away they were, the redder they became, being crisscrossed with crescents of black shadow all the way to the point where, merging into a single yellow grayness, they surrounded formidable slabs of bare volcanic rock jutting into the sky. He stood there and gazed while his men, unhurriedly, with movements automatized from years of practice, took their time-honored measurements, enclosing samples of air and sand in small containers, checking the radioactivity of the ground with a portable probe whose drilling mechanism was supported by the arctan. Rohan paid no attention to their toing and froing. His mask covered only his nose and mouth, while his eyes and the rest of his head were free, as he had taken off his small helmet. He felt the wind in his hair; tiny grains of sand settled on his face, tickling as they blew between his cheek and the plastic rim of the mask. Restless gusts set the pant legs of his jump suit flapping; the great, swollen-looking disk of the sun, which it may not have hurt to stare at for a second or so, now lay immediately behind the nose of the rocket. The wind whistled continuously: the force field did not affect the movement of gases, and so he was quite unable to spot where its invisible wall rose up out of the sand. The vast expanse he took in with his gaze was lifeless, as if no human had ever set foot on it, as if it were not the planet that had swallowed up another spaceship of the same class as the *Invincible*, with a crew of eighty, a huge, seasoned mariner of the void that was capable of releasing a billion megawatts of power in a split second and turning it into an energy field that could not be penetrated by any material body, or concentrating it into exterminating rays the temperature of the stars that could reduce a mountain chain to dust, or dry up an entire ocean. And yet that steel organism, built on earth, the fruit of centuries of technological progress, had perished here, in some unknown way, without a trace, without an SOS signal, as if it had melted into this gray-and-red wilderness.

And the entire continent looks the same, he thought to himself. He remembered clearly. From up above he had seen the pock-marks of the craters and the only movement that abided among them—the slow, unceasing drift of clouds hauling their shadows across the endless dunes.

"Activity?" he asked without turning around.

"Zero, zero and two," responded Jordan as he rose from his knees. His face had turned red and his eyes shone. The mask distorted his voice.

Which is to say, less than nothing, Rohan thought. Besides, the others wouldn't have perished from such a crude lack of caution; the automatic sensors would have sounded the alarm, even if no one had carried out the standard tests.

"Atmosphere?"

"Nitrogen seventy-eight percent, argon two percent, carbon dioxide zero, methane four percent. The rest is oxygen."

"Sixteen percent oxygen? Are you sure?"

"I'm sure."

"Radioactivity in the air?"

"Virtually zero."

That was strange. So much oxygen? This information galvanized him. He went up to the robot, which immediately presented him with a list of the readings. "Maybe they tried to go without oxygen equipment," he thought foolishly, for he knew that was impossible. True, it occasionally happened that some person especially tormented by homesickness would disobey orders and take off his mask, because the surrounding air would seem so pure, so fresh—and he would suffer from poisoning. But that could only happen to a single person, two at the most.

"Do you have everything?" he asked.

"Yes."

"Go back in then," he said to them.

"What about you, sir?"

"I'm going to stay awhile. Go back in," he repeated impatiently. He wanted to be alone now. Blank took the strap holding together the handles of the containers and slung it over his shoulder, Jordan gave the probe to the robot and they moved away, plodding with difficulty through the sand. The arctan paddled after them, looking from behind like another human in a mask.

Rohan went up to the furthest dune. From close up, poking out of the sand he saw the flared tip of one of the transmitters creating the force field. Not so much to check it was working, but rather on a childish whim he took a handful of sand and tossed it in front of him. It flew through the air and, as if encountering an unseen sloping pane of glass, scattered vertically to the ground.

His hands itched to take off the mask. He knew the feeling well. Spit out the plastic mouthpiece, yank off the straps, take a full breath of air, fill your lungs ...

"I'm losing it," he thought, and turned slowly back to the ship. The empty cage of the elevator was waiting for him, its platform gently immersed in the dune; during the few minutes he'd been absent the wind had already managed to coat it with a thin layer of sand.

Once he was in the main passageway of five deck he looked at the information screen on the wall. The commander was in the star cabin. He rode up.

"In a word, idyllic?" said the captain, summarizing what Rohan told him. "No radioactivity, no spores, bacteria, fungus, viruses, nothing—just the oxygen … Though of course we should run culture tests on the samples."

"The lab has them already. It may be that life developed on other continents here," said Rohan without conviction.

"I doubt it. Insolation outside the equatorial zone is poor; you saw the thickness of the polar caps, right? You can bet the covering of ice is at least five, even six miles deep. The ocean is more likely—algae, seaweed of some kind. But why didn't life come up onto the land?"

"We'll need to take a look at the water," said Rohan.

"It's too early to ask our people, but this looks like an old planet to me. A decrepit old egg like this has to be six billion years old. Not to mention that the sun is long past its prime. It's almost a red dwarf. Yes, the absence of life on land is striking. A particular kind of evolution that can't tolerate drought. Hm. That would explain the presence of oxygen, but not the matter of the *Condor*."

"Maybe there are forms of life, underwater beings, that are concealed in the ocean and have made a civilization down below," suggested Rohan. Both men studied a large Mercator projection map of the planet that lacked detail, since it had been drawn on the basis of data from unmanned probes in the previous century. It showed only the outlines of the principal continents and seas, the extent of the polar icecaps and a few of the largest craters. In the grid of intersecting lines of latitude and longitude there was a point circled in red at eight degrees north—the spot where they had landed. The captain shifted the map impatiently on the table.

"You don't believe it yourself," he objected. "Tressor couldn't have been more foolish than us, he wouldn't have let himself be overcome by something from underwater. That's nonsense. Besides, if intelligent aquatic beings had existed, one of the first things they would have done would be to conquer the land. Even in suits filled with water, let's say ... Utter nonsense," he repeated, not to put the final nail in the coffin of Rohan's idea, but because he was already thinking about something else.

"We'll stay here awhile," he concluded finally, and touched the lower edge of the map, which rolled up with a soft snap and disappeared into one of the horizontal drawers of the map case. "We'll wait and see."

"And if not?" Rohan inquired cautiously. "Will we go looking for them?"

"Be sensible, Mr. Rohan. Six star years later and this—" the captain sought the right expression, failed to find it, and instead made a dismissive gesture with his hand. "The planet is the size of Mars. How are we supposed to look for them? The *Condor*, that is," he corrected himself.

"Well, yes, the ground is ferrous," Rohan admitted reluctantly. In fact, the analyses had revealed a significant quantities of iron oxides in the sand. So ferroinductive detectors would be useless. Not knowing what to say, he remained silent. He was confident the captain would eventually find some way forward. After all, they couldn't return empty-handed, with nothing to show for their efforts. He waited, staring at Horpach's bushy eyebrows that stuck out from his forehead.

"Truth be told, I don't believe that waiting for 48 hours will do anything for us, though the regulations require it," the commander said in an unexpectedly confessional tone. "Have a seat, Mr. Rohan. You're standing over me like a bad conscience. Regis is the stupidest place you could imagine. Absolutely unnecessary. Who knows why the *Condor* was even sent here. Well, never mind that, since it already happened."

He broke off. He was in a bad mood, and as usual at such times he became talkative and was easily drawn into discussion, even on confidential topics, which was a little dangerous since at any moment he was capable of cutting the conversation short with some malicious comment.

"In a word, one way or another we have to do something. You know what? Send up a couple of small photo surveillance planes into orbit around the equator. Just make sure they follow a regular path, and tight in. Forty miles, say."

"That's inside the ionosphere," objected Rohan. "They'll burn up after a few dozen orbits."

"Let them. Before they do, they'll photograph everything that can be photographed. I'd even recommend you risk thirty-five miles. They may burn up after ten orbits, but only pictures from that close can serve any purpose. You know what a rocket looks like from sixty miles away, even with the best telephoto lens. A whole mountain looks like the head of a pin. Go right away and—Mr. Rohan!"

At this exclamation the navigator turned in the doorway. The commander threw the report from the analyses onto the table.

"What is this? It's idiotic. Who wrote it?"

"One of the automatons. What is it?" asked Rohan, trying to remain calm, because he too felt a rising anger. What's he found to complain about now, he thought, coming back into the room at a deliberately slow walk.

"Read this. Here, this part."

"Methane four percent." He himself was suddenly dumbstruck.

"Methane four percent, eh? And oxygen sixteen percent? You know what that means? It's a lethal combination! Can you explain why the entire atmosphere didn't explode when we were landing with boranes?"

"You're right, captain … I don't get it," stammered Rohan. He hurried to the exterior control console, took a little of the outside atmosphere in through the suction sensors, and while the captain paced around the bridge in ominous silence, Rohan watched the analyzers earnestly rattling their glass containers.

"Well?"

"The same. Methane four percent … oxygen sixteen," said Rohan. He had no idea how this was possible, it was true; at the same time, though, he felt a sense of satisfaction: At least now Horpach wouldn't be able to accuse him of having done bad work.

"Let me take a look! Methane four. Well I'll be … Fine. Mr. Rohan, get those probes up into orbit, then come to the small lab, if you please. What do we have scientists here for anyway? Let them worry their heads over it."

Rohan took the elevator down, summoned two rocket technicians and repeated the commander's orders. Then he went back up to two deck. Here were the laboratories and the specialists' cabins. He passed a series of narrow doors set into the metal wall, each bearing a plate with two letters: "C.E.," "C.P.," "C.T.," "C.B." and many more. The door of the small lab stood wide open; the captain's bass voice rose from time to time above the monotonous hum of the scientists' voices. Rohan stopped in the doorway. All the "Chiefs" were here— the Chief Engineer, Chief Biologist, Physicist, Physician, and all the technicians from the engine room. The captain was sitting, silent now, in the farthest chair, beneath the electronic programmer of a portable digital device, while olive-skinned Moderon, with folded arms that were as small as a little girl's, was saying:

"I'm not a specialist in gases. But in any case it's probably not regular methane. The energy of the bonds isn't the same; the difference is only in the second decimal place, but it's there. It doesn't react with oxygen except in the present of catalysts, and even then only reluctantly."

"What's the source of the methane?" asked Horpach. He was twiddling his thumbs.

"The carbon in it is for sure of organic origin. There isn't much of it, but there's no doubt."

"Are there isotopes? How old are they? What's the age of the methane?"

"From two to fifteen million years."

"That's quite a span!"

"We've only had half an hour. I can't say any more."

"Doctor Quastler! Where's the methane from?"

"I don't know."

Horpach looked from one specialist to another. It seemed he was about to explode, but all of a sudden he gave a smile.

"Gentlemen, you're all experienced scientists. We've been flying together now for how long. Please, tell me what you think. What are we to do now? Where should we begin?"

Since no one seemed eager to speak, the biologist Joppe, one of the few who were not afraid of Horpach's quick temper, looked the commander calmly in the eye and said:

"This is not a regular sub-delta-92 class planet. If it were, the *Condor* wouldn't have perished. Since it carried experts who were neither better nor worse than us, the one thing we know for certain is that their knowledge proved inadequate to avoid a disaster. That means we need to maintain degree three procedures, and run tests on the land and the ocean. I think we should commence geological drilling, and at the same time take a look at the water here. Anything else would be mere hypothesis, and in such a situation we can't allow ourselves that luxury."

"Very well." Horpach tightened his jaw. "Drilling within the perimeter of the force field isn't a problem. Dr. Nowik can oversee it."

The Chief Geologist nodded.

"As for the ocean . . . How far is the coastline, Mr. Rohan?"

"About a hundred twenty miles," said the navigator, not in the least surprised that the commander knew he was present, though he couldn't see him—Rohan was standing several feet behind him by the door.

"That's rather far. But we're not going to move the *Invincible* at this point. Take as many men as you see fit, Mr. Rohan— Fitzpatrick, or another oceanologist too, and six of the reserve energobots. Go to the shore. You will operate exclusively within a force field—no sorties onto the ocean, no diving. And be sparing with the automatons—we don't have that many of them. Is that all clear? You can begin. Oh, one other thing. Is the air here fit for breathing?"

The physicians consulted among themselves in whispers.

"In principle, yes," said Stormont eventually, though as if without particular conviction.

"What do you mean, 'in principle'? Can it be breathed or can it not?"

"These quantities of methane aren't a trivial matter. After a certain time the blood will become saturated, and that could produce certain minor brain symptoms. Confusion, for instance ... But such a thing would only happen after an hour, maybe a few hours."

"Would it not be enough to use some kind of methane filter?"

"No, commander. That is, it wouldn't be worth producing filters, because they'd need to be changed frequently; and besides, the percentage of oxygen is actually rather low. Personally I'm in favor of using breathing apparatus."

"Hm. You other gentlemen agree?"

Witte and Eldjarn nodded. Horpach rose to his feet.

"Very well, let's begin. Mr. Rohan! What's the situation with the probes?"

"We'll be launching them any moment now. Can I check the orbits before I head out?"

"You can."

Rohan left the lab, which was still filled with a buzz of voices. As he entered the bridge the sun was just setting. The flushed red rim of its disk, so dark it was almost purple, was peeking out from behind the jagged edge of the crater with unnatural distinctness. The sky, which in this part of the Galaxy was dense with stars, at the present moment seemed somehow magnified. Great constellations appeared shining in ever lower regions, swallowing up the desert that was vanishing in the darkness. Rohan contacted the satellite launch pad in the prow. The launch of the first pair of photosatellites had just been ordered. The next ones would go in an hour. The following morning, daytime and nighttime photographs of both hemispheres of the planet would give an image of the entire equatorial zone.

"One minute thirty-seven ... azimuth seven. Loading ... ," the singsong voice repeated over the loudspeaker. Rohan turned down the volume and swiveled in his chair to face the main console. He would never have admitted it to anyone, but he always enjoyed the play of lights when a probe was being launched on a planetary orbit. First the glowing ruby-red, white, and blue check lights of the boosters came on. Then the starter automaton growled into action. When its hum suddenly cut out, the entire hull of the cruiser shook slightly. At the same time the desert visible on the monitors lit up in a phosphoric glow. With a high-pitched roar that was strained in the extreme, a miniature projectile shot from the bow-mounted launcher, bathing the mother ship in a stream of flames. The light from the receding booster flashed across the sides of the dunes ever more faintly, till it faded completely. At this point the rocket itself could no longer be heard either. The console, on the other hand, was a riot of gleams. The elongated lights of the ballistic gauge leaped out of the gloom with frantic rapidity; the pearl-gray lamps of the remote control answered them reassuringly; then the signals indicating the successive discarding of burned-out casings came on like a colorful Christmas tree; and lastly, above the entire seething rainbow of lights a pure white rectangle came on, showing that the satellite had entered its orbit. In the middle of its glowing white surface was an indistinct patch of gray that quivered and formed into the number 41. That was the altitude of the satellite. Rohan checked the settings for the orbit one more time; both perigee and apogee were within the requisite limits. He had nothing more to do here. He glanced at the ship's clock, which showed eighteen hundred hours, then at the clock that now showed local time—eleven pm. He closed his eyes for a moment. He was pleased about the coming mission to the ocean. He liked to work independently. Now he was sleepy and hungry. He wondered for a moment whether it wouldn't be a good idea to take an energy tablet. But he decided it was enough to eat a regular supper. As he stood he realized how tired he was; this surprised him, and the surprise itself cleared his head a little. He took the elevator down to the mess. His new team was already there—two drivers of the hovercraft transporters, including Jarg, whom he liked for the latter's unfailing good humor. Fitzpatrick was also there with two of his colleagues, Broza and Koechlin. They were just finishing their supper when Rohan ordered hot soup, and took from a wall cabinet some bread and a bottle of non-alcoholic beer. He was carrying his tray over to the table when the floor shook slightly. The *Invincible* had just launched another satellite.

*

The commander did not permit them to travel by night. They set out at five am local time, before the sunrise. Because of the order of the convoy, which was dictated by necessity, and its problematic slowness, such an arrangement was known as a cortege. At front and back there were energobots creating an ellipsoidal force field for the protection of all the vehicles inside—all-purpose hovercraft, jeeps carrying the radio equipment and the radar, a field kitchen, a transporter with a self-assembling hermetic barracks, and a small direct-strike laser on caterpillar tracks that was referred to informally as the punch. Rohan took his place along with three of the scientists in the leading energobot; it was far from comfortable, as there was barely room for everyone, but at least it gave the impression of reasonably normal travel. The cortege had to move at the speed of its slowest vehicles, which were in fact the energobots. It was not an especially pleasurable ride. The caterpillar tracks snarled and screeched in the sand, the turbines whined like mosquitoes the size of elephants, conditioned air blasted from the grates immediately behind the travelers' heads, and the entire energobot rocked like a heavy boat on the waves. The black spire of the *Invincible* soon dropped below the horizon. For some time they traveled in the horizontal rays of the cold blood-red sun across an unvarying desert; gradually there was less and less sand, while sloping sheets of rock jutted out and had to be maneuvered around. The oxygen masks, along with the wail of the motors, disinclined them to conversation. They watched the horizon closely, but the view was unchanging— agglomerations of rock and huge weathered boulders. At one point the plain began to slope downwards, and at the bottom of a gentle basin they came across a narrow creek, half dried up, its water glistening with the reflection of the red dawn. The rocks extending in layers on either side of the stream indicated that at times it was significantly fuller. They stopped for a short moment to test the water. It was entirely clean, quite hard, and contained iron oxides and trace amounts of sulphides. They set off again, at a somewhat higher speed now, since the caterpillars could move smoothly across the rocky surface. Low cliffs rose to the west. The last vehicle was in permanent contact with the *Invincible*; its radar antennae turned as the radar operators sat glued to their monitors, adjusting their headsets and chewing on slices of concentrate. From time to time a rock was flung from underneath one of the hovercraft as though it had been picked up by a little whirlwind, and it skipped up the rocky hillside as if suddenly come to life. Then low, bare hills rose up in their path. Without stopping, they took some samples, and Fitzpatrick shouted to Rohan that the silica was of organic origin. Finally, when the surface of the ocean appeared before them as a blue-black line, they also found limestone. They drove down to the shore, crunching over small flat pebbles. The hot blast from the vehicles, the hiss of the caterpillar tracks, the whine of the turbines—everything abruptly fell silent when they were about a hundred yards from the ocean, which from close up looked greenish and very much resembled a terrestrial sea. Now it was time for a complex maneuver, for in order to protect the working group beneath a force field, the leading energobot needed to be moved a considerable distance into the water. After ensuring it was water-tight, it was guided into place remotely from the other energobot. It stirred up waves and foam till in the end it was no more than a dark, barely discernible spot far out on the surface; only then, at a signal from the command post, did the huge submerged machine elevate its Dirac transmitter; once the force field was in place, its invisible dome extending across part of the shore and the nearby waters, they began their tests.

The ocean was somewhat less saline than on Earth. But the tests produced nothing in the way of surprises. After two hours' work they knew more or less what they had when they started. They decided to send two remotely controlled televisual probes far out to sea, following their progress on monitors at the command post. It was only when the probes disappeared over the horizon that the signals sent the first important information. There were organisms resembling bony fish living in the ocean. At the sight of the probes, however, they fled at immense speed, seeking refuge in the depths. Echo sounders in the place where living beings were first encountered revealed the ocean to be five hundred feet deep.

Broza insisted on capturing at least one of the supposed fish. So they hunted them, the probes sending off electrical discharges as they pursued shadows twisting in the greenish murk. But the creatures were extraordinarily agile. It was only after firing multiple times that they succeeded in hitting one.

The probe seized it in its pincers and was immediately directed to return. In the meantime Koechlin and Fitzpatrick operated the other probe, gathering samples of fibers that floated far out on the water, and that they took to be some kind of local algae or seaweed. Finally they directed the probe all the way to the ocean bed, to a depth of eight hundred feet. A powerful underwater current at that depth made it extremely difficult to maneuver the probe, which kept drifting toward a large cluster of submerged rocks. In the end, however, they managed to move some of the rocks aside, and, as Koechlin had predicted, under this cover was an entire colony of supple, brush-like little creatures.

The two probes returned to the force field and the biologists went to work. In the barracks set up in the meantime, where it was at last possible to take off their cumbersome masks, Rohan, Jarg and the five other men ate their first hot meal of the day.

The time till evening was spent gathering mineral samples, testing levels of radioactivity near the ocean floor, taking insolation measurements, and a hundred other equally humdrum tasks that nevertheless had to be carried out conscientiously, pedantically even, if the results were to be valid. By nightfall everything that could be done, had been done, and Rohan could pick up the microphone with a clear conscience when Horpach called from the *Invincible*. The ocean was full of living forms, every one of which, however, avoided the coastal zone. The organism of the fish they had dissected had not revealed anything of particular interest. According to their preliminary estimates, evolution had been taking place on the planet for several hundreds of millions of years. Significant amounts of green algae had been found, which explained the presence of oxygen in the atmosphere. The division of living beings into plant and animal kingdoms was standard, as was the bone structure of the vertebrates. The only developed organ in the dissected fish for which the biologists knew of no terrestrial equivalent proved to be sensitive to very subtle changes in the intensity of magnetic fields. Horpach ordered the whole team to return as soon as possible and, just before bringing the conversation to a close, he said there was news: They had in all probability identified the place where the lost *Condor* had landed.

For this reason, despite the protests of the biologists, who asserted that even several weeks of further tests would be too little, the barracks was broken down, the motors started, and the column set off in a northwesterly direction. Rohan was unable to tell his traveling companions anything about the *Condor* because he himself knew nothing. He was eager to get back to the ship as soon as he could, because he guessed the commander would be assigning the next mission, which might be richer in discoveries. Now, of course, above all else he wished to explore the place where the *Condor* had supposedly landed. Rohan squeezed every drop of power from the vehicles, and they returned amid an even more hellish clatter of rocks crushed beneath caterpillar tracks. When night fell they turned on the huge headlights of the vehicles. It was an extraordinary, even sinister sight—at every other moment the roving beams of light picked out of the darkness the misshapen, seemingly mobile silhouettes of great giants that turned out to be only rocks that were the last lingering evidence of collapsed mountain chains. Several times they had to halt at deep crevasses yawning open in the basalt. In the end though, well after midnight, they caught sight of the trunk of the *Invincible*, lit up from all sides as if it were on parade, and gleaming from far off like a metal tower. Columns of vehicles were moving about in every direction within the force field: Fuel and supplies were being unloaded, while groups of men stood by the ramp in the blinding glare of floodlights. From far off those returning could hear the noises of the antlike bustle. Above the moving beams of the headlights rose the cruiser's silent, streaked hull. Blue flares were lit to indicate where an opening would appear in the force field, and one by one the vehicles, coated in a thick layer of fine dust, entered the circular space. Before he had even jumped to the ground, Rohan was already calling to one of the men standing close by, whom he recognized as Blank, to ask about the *Condor*.

But the bosun knew nothing about the alleged discovery. Rohan learned little from him. Before burning up in the denser strata of the atmosphere, the four satellites had provided eleven thousand photographs, transmitted by radio and printed on specially prepared plates in the map cabin as they came in. So as not to waste time, Rohan summoned the cartographic technician Erett and, as the former showered, he questioned the other man about everything that had happened on the ship. Erett was one of those who had been searching for the *Condor* on the series of photographs sent by the satellites. About thirty people were simultaneously looking for that grain of steel in an ocean of sand—along with the planetologists all the cartographers, radar operators, and the ship's pilots had been put to work. Twenty-four hours a day, in shifts they examined the incoming photographic materials, making a note of the coordinates of any questionable object. But the news that the commander had conveyed to Rohan turned out to be mistaken. What they had thought to be the ship was in fact an exceptionally tall pinnacle of rock that cast a shadow strangely reminiscent of that of a rocket. So as it turned out, it was still the case that nothing was known about what happened to the *Condor*. Rohan meant to report to his commander, but Horpach had already turned in, so he went to his own cabin. Despite his exhaustion, for a long time he was unable to fall asleep. When morning came, the captain sent Rohan an order via Ballmin, the head planetologist, to have all the materials they'd gathered brought to the main lab. At ten in the morning Rohan suddenly felt so hungry—he'd not eaten breakfast—that he took the elevator down to the radar operators' small mess on two deck. It was here, as he stood drinking coffee, that Erett found him.

"Do you have her?" he exclaimed, seeing the excited expression on the cartographer's face.

"No. But we've found something bigger. Come right away—the captain's sending for you."

The glass-cased cylinder of the elevator seemed to Rohan to be moving at a snail's pace. Silence reigned in the subdued lighting of the cabin; all that could be heard was the hum of electrical relays, while the machine spat out ever new, still damp photographs. But no one paid any attention to them. Two technicians had slid a kind of epidioscope from a hatch in the wall and were just turning off the last lights when Rohan opened the door. He could see the commander's white head among the others. The next moment a screen dropped from the ceiling and glowed silver. In the quiet of intent breathing Rohan moved as close as he could to the large bright surface. The picture was not of the best quality, and only black and white. In a ring of small craters dotted here and there, a bare plateau could be seen that on one side broke off with a line so straight it looked like the rock had been cut with an immense knife; this had to be the coast, as the rest of the image was filled with the uniform blackness of ocean. At a certain distance from the line there extended a mosaic of indistinct shapes which in two places were covered by a blur of clouds and their shadows. But even so there was no doubt that the bizarre, fuzzy formation was not a geological phenomenon.

A city ... Rohan thought in his excitement, but did not say it out loud. Everyone remained silent. The technician at the epidioscope was trying in vain to make the image sharper.

"Was there any static?" The commander's calm voice broke the silence.

"No," answered Ballmin from the darkness. "Reception was good, but this is one of the last pictures from satellite number three. Eight minutes after sending it, it stopped responding. The lenses were probably already damaged by the rising temperature."

"At the epicenter the camera was no higher than forty miles," added another voice that sounded to Rohan like Malte, one of the ablest of the planetologists. "Actually, I'd estimate it to be between thirty and thirty five. See here." His silhouette appeared against the screen. He took a clear plastic stencil in which circles were cut and placed it one after another against several of the craters in the other half of the picture.

"They're visibly larger than in the preceding images. Though in fact," he added, "that's neither here nor there. Either way ..."

He trailed off, but everyone understood what he was implying: that soon they would check the accuracy of the photograph since they would be exploring that part of the planet. They all stared a moment longer at the image on the screen. Rohan was no longer so sure it showed a city, or rather its ruins. The geometrically regular formation had long ago been abandoned, as could be told by the razor-thin, undulating shadows of the dunes, which had washed over the complex shapes from every direction till some of them were virtually submerged in the sandy deluge of the desert. Also, the geometric arrangement of the ruins was divided in two unequal parts by a zigzagging black line that broadened away from the coast. It was a seismic fissure that had split some of the larger "buildings" in two. One of them, which had clearly collapsed, formed a kind of bridge whose other end rested on the far rim of the cleft.

"Lights, please," came the voice of the commander. When they were turned on, he glanced at the wall clock.

"We leave in two hours."

A confusion of voices arose; the most energetic protests came from the Chief Biologist's team, who had reached a depth of six hundred fifty feet even in their test bores. Horpach gestured with his hand to indicate there would be no discussion.

"All the vehicles are to be brought back on board. Secure the materials we've gathered. The analysis of the photographs and the other tests are to continue as before. Where's Mr. Rohan? Oh, there you are. Good. Did you hear what I said? In two hours everyone is to be in takeoff positions."

The task of embarking the vehicles proceeded hastily but systematically. Rohan was deaf to the entreaties of Ballmin, who begged for fifteen more minutes' drilling.

"You heard what the commander said," he kept repeating left and right, hurrying the mechanics, who were driving up to the recently dug bore holes with huge cranes. In turn the drilling equipment, the makeshift gangways, the fuel canisters made their way into the cargo holds; when the uneven ground alone remained to mark the work that had been carried out, Rohan and Westergard, the Deputy Chief Engineer, made a final round of the area. Then the humans vanished into the ship. It was only now that the sands around the distant perimeter began to move. Summoned by radio, the energobots returned to the ship one by one, after which the ramp and the vertical shaft of the elevator retracted beneath the armor plating of the ship. There was a moment of stillness; then the monotonous whistling of the wind was drowned out by a metallic hiss of compressed air from the jets. The stern was swathed in billows of dust lit by a green glow that mingled with the red light from the sun, and, in a whirl of unceasing booms that rocked the desert and echoed back again and again from the rock walls, **33** the ship rose slowly into the air, leaving behind it a torched circle of rock, vitrified dunes and splashes of condensation, and receded with increasing velocity into the purple sky. For a long time afterwards, when the last trace of its path, marked by an off-white vapor trail, had melted away into the atmosphere, and the shifting sands had begun to cover the bare rock and fill the abandoned drilling shafts, from the west there appeared a dark cloud. Moving along close to the ground, it spread out; with a swirling extended arm it surrounded the landing site and hung there motionless. It remained there for some time. Then, when the sun had definitively dropped to the west, a black rain began to fall on the desert.

AMID THE RUINS

The *Invincible* landed at a carefully selected site almost three and a half miles to the north of the outer limits of the so-called city. It could be seen quite clearly from the bridge. The impression that these were artificially made constructions was even stronger than from viewing the satellite photographs. Angular, mostly wider at their base than higher up, of varying heights, they extended for several miles. They were blackish and in places gleamed metallically, but even the most powerful telescope was unable to make out details; most of the buildings appeared to be riddled with holes.

This time the creak of the cooling jets had not yet ceased when the ship extended the ramp and the scaffolding of the elevator, then surrounded itself with a ring of energobots. But the operation did not end there. In one place that lay directly opposite the city (at ground level it was hidden behind a range of low hills), within the force field a group of five rovers gathered; they were joined by another vehicle twice their size that resembled an apocalyptic beetle with a livid carapace: the mobile antimatter cannon.

The leader of the mission was Rohan. He stood erect on the first rover, in its open turret, waiting for the order from the *Invincible* that would open a passage through the force field. Two infobots on the closest hills sent up a series of long-action green flares to mark the route, and the small column moved forward two by two, with Rohan in the lead.

A deep hum came from the immense vehicles' engines, sand spraying from under their balloonlike wheels. Two hundred yards ahead of them, hovering over the surface was a scout robot that resembled a flattened bowl; its antennae twitched, while the streams of air that blew from underneath it played havoc with the crests of the dunes, making it seem that as it passed it lit an invisible fire within them. The wreaths of dust thrown up by the column drifted for the longest time in the still air, and the passage of the vehicles was marked by a reddish swirling trail. The shadows thrown by the column were longer and longer; the sun was about to set. They passed an almost completely sand-filled crater and in the space of twenty minutes reached the edge of the ruins. Here the formation broke up. The three unmanned craft moved outward, and bright blue lights came on to indicate they had created a local force field. The two manned vehicles continued on within the mobile shield. Fifty yards behind them the massive antimatter cannon followed on its jointed legs the height of a single-story building. At a certain moment, after they had crossed a submerged tangle of what looked like jumbled metal cables or wires, they had to stop because one limb of the cannon had fallen into an unseen gap beneath the sand. Two arctans dropped from the lead rover and freed the trapped giant. The convoy continued on its way.

The thing they had been calling a city was in reality nothing like any terrestrial settlement. Submerged to an unknown depth in shifting dunes were dark edifices with spiky, brushlike surfaces unlike anything the humans had ever laid eyes on. The shapes, which could not even be given an adequate name, were several stories high. They had no windows, doors, walls even; some looked like densely tangled nets folded over and crisscrossing one another in every direction, with thicker points at the places where they intersected; others recalled complex spatial arabesques of a kind that might be made by mutually interpenetrating honeycombs, or sieves with three- or five-sided holes. In every larger element and every visible plane some kind of regularity could be perceived; it was not as homogeneous as that of a crystal, say, but was undeniable, repeating in a definite rhythm, though it was interrupted in many places by signs of disintegration. Some of the constructions were made from broken-off angular branches that had twisted together (though the branches themselves did not have the freedom of growth possessed by a tree or bush, rather they either constituted part of an archway or two spirals turning in opposite directions). These structures jutted vertically out of the sand, though the visitors also noticed others that inclined at an angle like the arm of a drawbridge. The wind, which blew most frequently from the north, had covered all the horizontal places and some of the shorter overhangs with a fine sand, such that from a distance a number of the ruins resembled squat pyramids with their tops cut off. From close up, however, the seemingly smooth surface revealed what it really was: a system of shaggy, pointed rods and slats that in places were so enmeshed they retained sand in their midst. To Rohan they looked like some kind of cubic or pyramidal remains of rocks that had been overgrown with vegetation now dead and dry. But this impression too dissipated from closer up: At that moment a regularity foreign to living forms revealed its presence despite the chaos of deterioration. The ruins were not actually solid, as you could look into them through gaps in the metal snarl; nor were they empty, as the tangle filled them through and through. The whole place exuded an emptiness devoid of life. Rohan thought of the antimatter cannon, but there was no point in using force since there was no interior it would have enabled them to enter. The gale drove billows of stinging dust between the tall bastions. The regular mosaics of black openings were slowly being filled with sand that continually seeped in, forming steep little cones around their bases like miniature landslides. The entire time they were there, they were accompanied by a ceaseless rustle of drifting sand. The spinning antennae, the needles of the portable Geiger counters, the ultrasonic microphones, the radiation sensors—all were silent. All that could be heard was the crunch of sand under the wheels, the intermittent whine of the engines as they changed formation at turns. The column alternately dipped into the deep cool shadow cast by successive edifices, then remerged onto the sand that was bright red in the sunlight.

They eventually reached the tectonic fissure. It was an opening about a hundred yards wide that seemed bottomless and was certainly extremely deep, because it had not been filled by the cascades of sand being continually swept over the side by gusts of wind. They came to a halt, and Rohan dispatched a flying robot scout to the other side. On the monitor he watched what the device could capture with its television cameras, but the image only showed more of what they had already seen. The scout was summoned back within an hour; when it arrived, Rohan consulted with Ballmin and with the physicist Gralev, who were sitting in his vehicle, and decided to explore some of the ruins more closely.

He first attempted to use an ultrasound probe to determine the depth of the layer of sand covering the "streets" of this dead city. It was laborious work. Successive soundings yielded contradictory results, probably because the bedrock had been subject to internal decrystalization in the course of the shock that caused the immense crack. The whole vast trough-shaped depression appeared to be filled with twenty to thirty feet of sand. They headed east, toward the ocean; taking a winding route between the blackish ruins, which rose ever lower, buried deeper and deeper in the sands till eventually nothing could be seen, they arrived at an area of sandless rock. They stopped there, on a clifftop so high the sound of the waves breaking against its base reached them as a barely audible whisper. This strip of naked rock, unnaturally smooth, marked the line of the cliffs, rising to the north in a series of peaks that leapt in motionless bounds into the mirror of the ocean.

They had left the city behind them—it appeared now as a black regularly shaped line plunged in a ruddy mist. Rohan contacted the *Invincible*, informed the commander of what they had learned—which was essentially nothing—and the entire column, continuing to exercise every means of caution, returned to the heart of the ruins.

Along the way they had a small accident. The energobot farthest to the left, probably because of a minor directional error, broadened the force field too far and caused it to brush up against the edge of a honeycombed, tapering edifice leaning towards them. Someone had set the antimatter cannon to fire automatically in case of attack; it was connected to the indicators from the force field and, interpreting the jump in power as an unambiguous sign that someone was trying to break through the field, it fired at the innocent ruin. The whole upper section of the crooked building, the height of a terrestrial skyscraper, was set aglow; its previously dirty black color

39

was replaced with blinding light, then a split second later it disintegrated in a shower of boiling metal. Not a single fragment fell on the column, as the flaming debris slid down the domed surface of the invisible shield, evaporating from the thermic shock before it hit the ground. But the blast caused a jump in radioactivity, the Geiger counters automatically sounded the alarm, and Rohan, cursing and vowing to break the bones of whoever had programmed the cannon, lost a good deal of time in calling off the alarm and responding to the *Invincible*, which had spotted the flash and immediately asked what was going on.

"For now, all we know is that it's metal. Probably steel alloyed with tungsten and nickel," said Ballmin, who, paying no attention to the hustle-bustle around him, had taken the opportunity to carry out a spectroscopic analysis of the flames engulfing the ruin.

"Can you estimate how old it is?" asked Rohan, wiping off the fine grains of sand that had settled on his hands and face. They left behind them what was left of the ruin, twisted by the heat; it now leaned over their path like a broken wing.

"No. I can tell you it's a hell of an age. A hell of an age," he repeated.

"We need to take a closer look. And I'm not going to ask the old man for permission," added Rohan with sudden determination.

They pulled up next to a complex structure formed by a series of arms that came together in the center. A portal opened in the force field, marked by two flares. From close up, the predominant impression was of confusion. The facade of the building was composed of triangular plates linked by wire "brushes"; from inside the plates were supported by a system of rods as thick as tree branches. At the surface things looked more or less orderly, but deep within, when they tried to see in using powerful flashlights, the forest of rods forked, spreading from thick nodes, then joined together again. The whole construction resembled a massive wireworks, a seething tangle of millions of cables. They scoured it for signs of electric current, polarization, traces of magnetic field, and radioactivity. Nothing showed up.

The green flares indicating the entrance to the force field flickered restlessly. The wind whistled; the masses of air driven into the steel thickets made bizarre singing noises.

"What does it mean, this damn jungle?"

Rohan wiped his face; sand was sticking to the sweat on his skin. He and Ballmin were standing by the guard rail on the superstructure of a flying recon craft that was hovering fifty feet or so above a "street," or rather a three-sided square covered in sand, between two ruins inclining toward one another. Far below were their vehicles; the humans tipping their heads back to watch them were as small as toy figurines.

The recon craft moved on. They now found themselves over a surface comprising innumerable spiky blades of blackish metal; it was uneven, ragged, and in places covered with triangular plates that were not lying flat: Angled upwards or to the side, they made it possible to see into the dark interior. The mesh of intertwined partitions, rods, honeycombed concavities was so dense that sunlight could not get through; the beams of the flashlights were equally useless.

"What do you think, Dr. Ballmin? What can all this mean?" repeated Rohan. He was feeling exasperated. His forehead was red from continually being wiped; his skin was sore, his eyes were stinging, in a few minutes he was due to send in another report to the *Invincible*, yet he couldn't even find words to describe what he was seeing.

"I'm no clairvoyant," the scientist came back. "I'm not even an archeologist. Though actually I don't think an archeologist would be able to tell you anything either. If you ask me—" He broke off.

"Spit it out!"

"These don't look to me like residential structures. Like the ruins of living quarters of any beings, you see what I'm saying? If it can be compared to anything, it would be machinery."

"Machinery, huh? But what kind? Something that gathers information? Maybe it was some kind of computer?"

"I doubt you believe that yourself," retorted the planetologist levelly.

The craft moved sideways, still close to touching the rods that stuck out chaotically from among the twisted plates.

"No. There were no electric circuits here. Do you see any cells, insulators, shields?"

"Perhaps they were flammable. They could have been destroyed by fire. After all, these are ruins," Rohan replied without conviction.

"Perhaps," Ballmin unexpectedly agreed.

"So what am I to tell the commander?"

"You'd be better off just sending him televisual images of the whole kit and caboodle."

"This wasn't a city," Rohan said suddenly, as if he were mentally summing up everything he'd seen.

"Probably not," nodded the planetologist. "In any case, not the kind we're capable of imagining. No humanoid beings lived here, nothing that even vaguely resembled us. Whereas the oceanic life forms look very much like terrestrial ones. So you'd expect to find them on land too."

"Right. I keep thinking about that. None of the biologists are willing to talk about it. What are your thoughts?"

"They're unwilling to talk about it because it smacks of the improbable: It looks as though something refused to allow life on the land ... as if it prevented it from leaving the water ..."

"A cause like that could have come into effect on one single occasion, for instance in the form of a supernova explosion very close by. After all, as you know, Zeta Lyrae was a nova millions of years ago. Perhaps hard radiation killed off life on the continents, while organisms living deep in the ocean were able to survive ..."

"If the radiation were as powerful as you say, signs of it would be evident even today. Whereas ground radioactivity is unusually low for this part of the Galaxy. Besides, through those millions of years evolution would have moved forward; there wouldn't be any vertebrates, of course, but you'd see primitive life forms along the coast. Did you notice that the shore is completely devoid of life?"

"I did. Is that really so significant?"

"It's crucial. Life generally begins in the coastal zone, and only later moves out into the deep ocean. Things couldn't have been any different here. Something pushed it away. And I believe that to this day it's not allowing access to the land."

"Why do you think so?"

"Because the fish were afraid of our probes. On the planets I'm familiar with, no animals were ever afraid of our devices. They never fear something they haven't ever previously seen."

"Are you suggesting they've seen probes before?"

"I don't know what they've seen. But why would they need a magnetic sense?"

"Damn this whole business!" growled Rohan. Staring at the tattered festoons of metal, he leaned over the guard rail. The twisted black ends of the rods quivered in the column of air blowing from the craft. With a long-handled pair of pliers, Ballmin snipped off the ends of the wires jutting from the tunnel-shaped opening.

"I'll tell you one thing," he said. "The temperature here was never even particularly high, otherwise the metal would have fused. So your hypothesis of a conflagration also has to be rejected ..."

"Every hypothesis fails here," muttered Rohan. "On top of which, I can't see the connection between this crazy tangle and the disappearance of the *Condor*. I mean, all this is completely inanimate."

"It wasn't necessarily always that way."

"A thousand years back, sure, but not just a few years ago. There's no point in searching this place any longer. Let's go back down."

They spoke no more till the craft had touched down by the green signal lights of the expedition. Rohan instructed the technicians to turn on the TV cameras and transmit data to the *Invincible*.

He himself sat behind closed doors in the cabin of the main transporter, with the scientists. Once they had blown oxygen into the tiny space, they set about eating sandwiches, washing them down with coffee from thermos flasks. An illuminated tube shone overhead. Rohan found its white light agreeable. He had come to dislike the planet's red daylight. Ballmin spat:

Sand that had crept under his mask was gritting between his teeth as ate.

"This reminds me of something," said Gralev unexpectedly as he screwed his flask shut. His thick black hair glistened in the fluorescent glow. "I'll tell you, but only if you promise not to take it too seriously."

"If it reminds you of anything at all, that's already a big deal," replied Rohan through a mouthful of food. "Tell us what it is."

"It's not something I experienced directly. But I heard this story … Well, it's more a kind of fable. About the Lyrans."

"That's not a fable. They really existed. Akhramian has a whole monograph about them," Rohan put in. Behind Gralev's back a light on the console began to blink, indicating they had direct contact with the *Invincible*.

"Right. Payne reckoned that some of them managed to survive. But I'm almost certain that isn't true. They all perished during the nova."

"That's sixteen light years from here," said Gralev. "I don't know Akhramian's book. But somewhere, I don't recall where, I heard a story of how they tried to save themselves. Apparently they sent spaceships to all the planets of other stars in their vicinity. They were already skilled at sub-lightspeed travel."

"And?"

"That's pretty much it. Sixteen light years isn't such a great distance. Maybe one of their ships landed here?"

"You think they might be here? Their descendants, that is?"

"I don't know. It's just that these ruins made me think of them. They could have built them …"

"What did they look like, actually?" asked Rohan. "Were they humanoid?"

"Akhramian thought so," replied Ballmin. "But it was only a hypothesis. Even less remained of them than of Australopithecus."

"Strange..."

"Not at all. Their planet was plunged in the chromosphere of the nova for thousands of years. At times the surface temperature exceeded ten thousand degrees. Even the bedrock of the planet's crust underwent a complete metamorphosis. The oceans vanished without a trace, the entire globe burned up like a bone. Imagine a hundred centuries inside the inferno of a nova!"

"Lyrans here? But why would they hide? And where?"

"Maybe they're all dead now? Besides, don't expect too much of me. I was only sharing something that occurred to me."

Silence fell. An alarm light flashed on the main console. Rohan jumped to his feet and donned a pair of headphones.

"Rohan here ... What? Is that you, sir? Yes! Yes! I'm listening ... Very well, we'll be back immediately!" He turned to the others, his face suddenly pale.

"The other team has found the Condor—a hundred eighty miles from here ..."

CONDOR

From a distance the rocket looked like a crooked tower. The impression was heightened by the surrounding dunes: The western rampart of sand was much higher than the eastern one, because of the direction of the prevailing winds. A number of tractors in the vicinity were almost completely buried; even the immobilized antimatter cannon, its hatch raised, was half immersed in sand. But the rear jets could still be seen, as the stern was located in a hollow protected from the wind. Thanks to this, it was enough to wipe away a thin layer of sand to reach the objects scattered around the ramp.

The men from the *Invincible* came to a stop at the edge of the rampart. The vehicles that had brought them already formed a broad ring around the whole area, and the bundles of rays they emitted had joined into a force field. They had left the transporters and infobots a hundred feet or so from the place where the sand had circled the base of the *Condor*, and they were looking from the top of the dune.

The ramp was suspended about twenty feet from the ground, as if something had stopped it from going further as it was being lowered. The framework of the personnel elevator was firmly in place, however, and the empty cage seemed to invite them in. Next to it, a number of oxygen canisters stuck out of the sand. Their aluminum sides gleamed as if they'd been dropped only moments before. A little further off, a light blue object poked from the dune; it turned out to be a plastic container. In fact, there was a multitude of objects scattered in disarray across the hollow at the base of the ship: jars of conserves, both full and empty; theodolites; cameras; telescopes; tripods; and mess kits—some intact, some bearing signs of damage.

It looked for all the world like someone had thrown armfuls of them from the rocket, thought Rohan to himself, tipping his head back to gaze at the dark opening of the personnel hatchway, its cover ajar. One of de Vries's small recon planes had come across the ship entirely by chance. De Vries had not attempted to enter the *Condor*, but had immediately radioed base. Rohan's team would be the first to investigate the mystery of the *Invincible*'s double. The technicians were already running up from their vehicles, toolkits in hand.

Noticing a bulging shape covered by a shallow layer of sand, Rohan turned it over with the tip of his boot, thinking it to be some kind of small globe, and, still not realizing what it was, picked the pale, yellowish sphere up from the ground. He gasped; everyone turned to look at him. He was holding a human skull.

After that they found other bones and many fragments, and also one complete skeleton in a jump suit. The mouthpiece of an oxygen mask still rested between the drooping lower jaw and the upper teeth; the pressure dial was stuck at 46 atmospheres. Jarg knelt down and turned the valve on the canister; gas came out with a prolonged hiss. In the perfectly dry air of the desert the steel parts of the pressure regulator were entirely untouched by corrosion, and the knobs turned easily.

The elevator mechanism could be operated from the cage, but the electricity was clearly not working, as pushing the buttons had no effect. Climbing up the forty-meter high structure presented quite a challenge, and Rohan wondered whether to send up a handful of men in a flying craft; but in the meantime two of the technicians had secured themselves with rope and were clambering up the frame. The others followed their progress in silence.

The *Condor*, a ship of the exact same class as the *Invincible*, had left the yard only a few years earlier, and in outline they could not be told apart. No one said anything. Though it had never been expressed in words, they may well have preferred to find shattered remnants left after an accident—even an explosion of the reactor. Everyone was stunned by the fact that the ship was simply standing there, sticking out of the desert sands, tilting lifelessly to one side as if the ground had given way beneath the stanchions of the stern, surrounded by a welter of objects and human bones, yet at the same time seemingly untouched. The climbers reached the personnel hatch, opened it without difficulty, and vanished from view. They were gone for such a long time that Rohan began to be concerned, but all of a sudden the elevator cage shuddered, rose three feet, then returned down onto the sand. At the same time the silhouette of one of the technicians appeared in the opening above; he gestured to indicate that they could come up.

Four men made the trip: Rohan, Ballmin, the biologist Hagerrup, and Kralik, one of the technicians. Out of habit Rohan studied the powerful curve of the ship's hull across the guard rail of the elevator and, for the first time that day, though not the last, he was dumbstruck. The titanium-molybdenum plates of the outer casing had been bored or pierced in multiple places with some terrifyingly hard device; the marks were not especially deep, but so closely spaced that the entire outer body of

49

the ship was dotted with them. Rohan shook Ballmin's shoulder to draw his attention to it, but Ballmin had already noticed this astounding thing. The two of them tried to take a closer look at the irregularities stippling the plating. They were all small, as if made with the sharp tip of a chisel, but Rohan knew that no chisel existed capable of denting the riveted surface. It could only be the result of some chemical process. But he had no time to figure it out, as the elevator came to the end of its short ascent and they had to enter the airlock.

Inside the ship the lights were on: The technicians had already started up the emergency generator, which worked on compressed air. The sand, unusually fine and loose, lay deep only in the immediate vicinity of the tall sill. The wind had blown it in through the cracked-open hatch cover. It had not gotten into the passageways. The interior of three deck opened to the newcomers, clean, tidy, brightly lit, with only the occasional object lying abandoned on the floor—an oxygen mask, a plastic plate, a book, part of a space suit. But that was only three deck. Lower down, in the cartography cabins and the star cabins, in the messes, in the crews' quarters, the radar rooms, in the main engine room, the passageways of the various decks and the gangways between them, there was incomprehensible chaos.

On the bridge they found an even more terrifying picture. Not one glass monitor screen or dial face was intact, it seemed. Furthermore, since all the glass was shatterproof, some kind of unbelievably powerful blows had turned it into a silvery powder that covered the consoles, the chairs, even the cables and switches. The adjoining library looked as if a big sack of buckwheat had been tipped out on the floor. It was littered with microfilm, much of it unspooled and tangled into big slithery wads. There were torn books, broken compasses and slide rules, scattered spectral and analytic tapes, along with piles of Cameron's huge star catalogues, which someone had especially mistreated, furiously yet with an incomprehensible patience ripping out their thick, stiff plastic pages one by one. In the clubroom and the projection room next to it the way was blocked by heaps of crumpled clothing and scraps of leather torn from the ripped upholstery of the armchairs. In a word, as the bosun Terner put it, it looked like the rocket had been set **51** upon by a troop of rabid monkeys. As they moved from one deck to the next, the men were left speechless at the sight of all this destruction. In the small navigation cabin, against the wall, curled into a ball lay the desiccated remains of a man in linen pants and stained shirt. The body had been covered with a tarpaulin by one of the technicians, who had been the first to enter the cabin. It was effectively mummified, its skin brownish and clinging to the bone.

Rohan was one of the last to leave the *Condor*. His head was spinning; he felt physically sick, and it took all his willpower to suppress a rising nausea. He felt as if he'd just had a terrible, unbelievable nightmare. Yet the faces of those around him confirmed the reality of what he had seen. They sent brief radiograms to the *Invincible*. Part of the team remained at the deserted *Condor* with the aim of bringing some sort of order to the ship's interior. Beforehand, however, Rohan ordered them to photograph all the cabins extensively, and to write detailed descriptions of the state in which they were found.

He set off back with Ballmin and Gaarb, one of the biophysicists. The driver of the transporter was Jarg. His broad, usually smiling face seemed to have shrunken and darkened. The vehicle, which weighed several tons, bounced up and down in a way quite unlike Jarg's usual steady handling; it zigzagged through the dunes, sending up huge sprays of sand on either side. In front of them was an unmanned energobot, providing a force field. They were silent the whole way, each of them thinking his own thoughts. Rohan was almost afraid to meet with the commander; he didn't really know what to tell him. One of the most terrible discoveries, because it had also been one of the most incomprehensible, he had kept to himself: In a bathroom on eight deck he had found bars of soap bearing the clear marks of human teeth. Yet they could not have suffered hunger there. The stores were filled with almost untouched supplies of food; even the milk in the refrigerators was still good.

Half way back to base, they received radio signals from a small driverless vehicle that was speeding towards them, trailing a wall of dust behind it. There were two passengers, the aging technician Magdow and Sax, a neurophysiologist. Rohan turned off the force field so they could communicate by voice. After he had left the *Condor*, a frozen human body had been found in the hibernation chamber. It was possible the man could still be brought back to life, so Sax had with him all the necessary equipment from the *Invincible*. Rohan decided to travel back with him, using the argument that the scientist's vehicle lacked force field protection. In reality, though, he was glad his conversation with Horpach would be postponed. They turned around and sped off amid billows of sand.

There was a bustle of activity around the *Condor*. All kinds of objects were still being found buried in the sand. In a separate place, under white tarpaulins, lay a row of human bodies; over twenty had been found so far. The ramp was working; even the *Condor's* stationary reactor was producing electricity. They were spotted from far off, from the clouds of dust they made, and the force field was opened to allow them through. A physician was already present—the diminutive Dr. Nygren—but he was unwilling to even begin an examination of the man found in the hibernation chamber without others being present. Rohan took advantage of his privilege—he was representing the commander himself on this mission—and joined the two medical men on board. The smashed objects that previously had prevented access even to the door of the hibernation chamber had in the meantime been cleared away. The gauges read one degree Fahrenheit. Seeing this, the two doctors exchanged knowing glances without saying anything, but Rohan knew enough about hibernation to be aware that such a temperature was too high for full reversible death, but too low for hypothermic sleep. It did not seem as if the man in the hibernation chamber had been prepared to survive in specially created conditions, but rather had found himself there by chance, in a way that was just as unaccountable and nonsensical as anything else they had seen on the *Condor*. And indeed, when they had donned their thermostatic suits and, turning the circular locks, opened the heavy door, they saw the body of a man dressed only in his underwear, lying spreadeagled on the floor. Rohan helped the physicians lift him onto a small padded table under three shadowless lamps. It wasn't exactly an operating table, but a sort of bed for the kinds of minor procedures that sometimes need to be carried out in a hibernation chamber. Rohan had been afraid to see the man's face, as he knew a good many of the *Condor's* crew. But this person was unfamiliar to him. Were it not for the freezing cold and the stiffness of his limbs, he could have been thought to be sleeping. His eyes were closed; in the dry air of the hermetic room his skin had retained its natural color, though it was pale. But the tissue beneath it was filled with microscopic ice crystals. The two doctors again exchanged meaningful glances without speaking. They began to prepare their instruments. Rohan sat on one of the empty bunks. The two long rows of them were all tidily made up. The hibernation room was perfectly orderly. The instruments clinked from time to time, the doctors murmured to one another, then finally Sax said as he moved away from the table:

"Nothing can be done."

"He's dead," said Rohan, rather drawing the only possible conclusion from the doctor's words than asking a question. In the meantime Nygren went up to the A/C control panel. After a short while, warm air began to blow. Rohan stood up, intending to leave, when he saw Sax return to the table, pick up a small black case from the floor and open it, revealing a piece of equipment that Rohan had heard of often but never seen used. With fastidious, uncommonly composed movements, Sax unwound reels of wire ending in flat electrodes. Attaching six of them to the dead man's skull, he fastened them in place with sticking tape. He squatted down and took three pairs of headphones from the case. He put one pair on and, still bending down, adjusted the knobs of the apparatus that was inside the case. His eyes were closed, and his face took on an expression of absolute concentration. All of a sudden he frowned, leaned even closer in, held one of the knobs in place with his hand, then snatched off his headphones.

"Dr. Nygren," he said in a strangely altered voice. The short physician took the headphones from him.

"What is it?" Rohan whispered almost without breathing, his lips trembling. The apparatus was known as a "grave-sounder," at least in ship's jargon. Immediately after someone had passed away, or if the body had not begun to decompose, as was the case here because of the low temperature, it was possible to "listen to the brain," or more precisely, whatever had been the last contents of its consciousness.

The device sent electrical impulses into the depths of the brain; they moved along the pathways of least resistance—which is to say, the nerve fibers that had formed a functional whole in the period immediately before decease. The results could never entirely be trusted, but there were rumors that in a number of cases information of the greatest weight had been gleaned in such a manner. In circumstances like the present, where so much depended on unraveling the mystery that shrouded the tragedy of the *Condor*, the use of the "grave-sounder" was a necessity. Rohan had already guessed that the neurologist hadn't even been counting on being able to revive the frozen man, and had really only come so as to hear what his brain would be able to tell him. He stood without moving, his mouth strangely dry and his heart pounding, as Sax handed him another pair of headphones. If it hadn't been for the simplicity and naturalness of this gesture, he would have lacked the courage to put them on. But he did so under Sax's steady, solemn gaze as the latter knelt on one knee by the apparatus, tweaking the knobs of the amplifier.

To begin with he heard nothing but the hum of current, and in fact felt relieved at this, since he did not wish to hear anything at all. Without even being aware of it, he would have preferred it if the brain of this unknown man had been as mute as a rock. Sax rose from the floor and straightened the headphones on Rohan's head. Then Rohan saw something through the light bathing the white wall of the room: a gray image, seemingly

55

made of loose ash, hazy and suspended in an undefined distance. He closed his eyes involuntarily and what he had seen a moment before became somewhat clearer. It looked like a passageway inside the ship, with pipes running along the overhead. It was blocked from one side to the other by human bodies. They appeared to be moving, but in fact the entire picture was shaking and rippling. The people were half naked; what was left of their clothing hung in tatters, and their unnaturally white skin was covered in something like black marks or some kind of rash. That too may have been an incidental effect of the image, since the floor and walls also teemed with the same black comma-shaped dots. The entire scene, like a blurred photograph taken through a thick layer of running water, trembled and undulated, stretching and shrinking. Rohan opened his eyes, overcome with horror; the picture darkened and almost vanished, merely casting a shadow over the bright light of the surrounding reality. But Sax turned the knobs of the apparatus again and Rohan heard, as if inside his own head, a faint whisper: "Ala ... ama ... lala ... ala ma ... mama ..."

And nothing further. The amplifier gave a sudden mewl, buzzed, and filled the headphones with a squeaking noise like a crazy hiccupping. It sounded like wild laughter, mocking and terrible. But it was merely the electric current—the heterodyne had begun to oscillate too powerfully ...

Sax wound up the wires, put them together and stowed them in the case. Nygren lifted the edge of the sheet and draped it over the body and face of the dead man. The latter's hitherto closed mouth, perhaps because of the heat—it was almost hot in the hibernation chamber by now, in any case Rohan's forehead was dripping with sweat—his mouth, then, opened slightly, giving him an expression of extreme surprise. And, still looking that way, it disappeared beneath the shroud . . .

"Say something . . . Why aren't you saying anything?" Rohan burst out. Sax tightened the straps of the case, stood up, and took a step towards him.

"Please be calm, Navigator Rohan . . ."

Rohan narrowed his eyes and clenched his fists; his effort was as immense as it was ineffective. As usually happened at such moments, fury rose inside him. That was the hardest thing to control.

"I'm sorry," he mumbled. "So what does all this actually mean?"

Sax unfastened the heavy suit, which slipped to the floor, and ceased to look large. Once again he was a small, stooping man with a sunken chest and slender, nervous hands.

"I know no more than you," he replied. "Perhaps even less."

Rohan understood nothing, but he latched on to Sax's last comment.

"What are you saying? Why even less?"

"Because I wasn't here—I've not seen anything except this body. You were on the *Condor* all day. Did that image not mean anything to you?"

"No. Those people—they were moving. Were they still alive then? What was on them? Those marks . . ."

"They weren't moving. That was an illusion. Engrams are recorded like a photograph. Sometimes there's a composite of several images, though not in this case."

"But what about the marks? Was that an illusion too?"

"I can't say. Anything is possible. But I don't believe so. What do you think, Dr. Nygren?"

The short doctor was already free of his thermostatic suit.

"I don't know," he said. "It may not even have been an arte-fact. There weren't any of them on the overhead, right?"

"The marks? No. Just on them ... and on the floor. And a few on the walls ..."

"If it had been a secondary projection, they'd probably have covered the whole picture," said Nygren. "But it's not certain. There's too much unpredictability in such recordings."

"What about the voice? That—that gibbering?" Rohan went on in desperation.

"One word was clear: 'mama.' You heard it?"

"Yes. But there were other things too. 'Ala' ... 'lala' ... it kept repeating."

"It was repeating because I was scanning the entire parietal cortex," murmured Sax. "In other words, the whole area of auditory memory," he explained to Rohan. "That was the most extraordinary thing of all ..."

"The words?"

"No, not the words. A dying man may think of anything; it would be quite normal for him to think about his mother. But his auditory memory was empty. Completely empty, you understand?"

"No, I don't understand a thing. What do you mean, empty?"

"Usually a scan of the parietal lobe is unhelpful," explained Nygren. "There are too many engrams in there, too many recorded words. It's as if you were trying to read a hundred books at once. It amounts to chaos. But this man," he said, looking at the elongated shape under the white sheet—"he had nothing there. No words except for those few syllables."

"That's right, I went from the sensory speech center all the way to the Rolandic fissure," said Sax. "That's why the syllables kept repeating, they were the last phonetic structures to survive."

"And the rest? The others?"

"They're not there." Sax seemed to lose patience, and jerked the heavy case from the floor, making the leather handle creak. "They're simply not there, that's all there is to it. Please don't ask me what happened to them. This man lost his auditory memory."

"What about the image?"

"That's another matter. He saw it. He may not even have understood what he was looking at, but a camera doesn't understand anything either, and it still records whatever it's pointed at. Though actually I have no idea whether he understood or not."

"Will you help me, Dr. Sax?"

The two physicians left with their equipment. The door closed. Rohan remained alone. At this moment he was overcome by such despair that he went up to the table, lifted the sheet, tossed it aside and, unbuttoning the dead man's shirt, which had thawed and was now entirely soft, examined his chest closely. He started when he first touched it, because even the skin had become springy; as the tissues thawed, the muscles had gone limp and the head, which had been raised unnaturally, lowered yieldingly as if the man were truly sleeping.

Rohan searched his body for signs of some mysterious epidemic, poisoning, bites; but he found nothing. Two fingers on the left hand had eased apart, revealing a small wound. Its edges were slightly turned back; the wound began to bleed. Red drops fell on the white foam padding of the table. This was too much for Rohan. Without even replacing the shroud on the dead man, he ran from the chamber, pushing past the people gathered outside, and headed for the main hatch as if he was being chased.

Jarg stopped him by the airlock, helped him put on an oxygen mask, even stuck the mouthpiece between his lips.

"No news, sir?"

"No, Jarg. Nothing. Nothing!"

He didn't notice who he rode down with in the elevator. The engines of the vehicles were whining. The wind was up, and waves of sand flew by, lashing at the pocked, uneven surface of the hull. Rohan had forgotten completely about this phenomenon. He went up to the stern, rose on tiptoe and gently touched the thick metal. The plating was like rock—exactly like an ancient, worn rock surface, covered with hard lumpy irregularities. Between the transporters he spotted the tall figure of Ganong the engineer, but he didn't even try to ask him what he thought about it. The engineer knew as much as he did. Which is to say, nothing. Nothing.

He returned with several people, sitting in the cabin of the biggest transporter. He heard their voices as if from a great distance. Terner the bosun was saying something about poisoning, but he was shouted down.

"Poisoned? With what? All the filters were in perfect shape! The oxygen reservoirs were full. Water supplies were untouched . . . They had all the food you could want . . ."

"You saw what that guy looked like that we found in the little navigation cabin?" asked Blank. "I knew him . . . I wouldn't have recognized him, but he wore this signet ring . . ."

No one responded. When Rohan got back to base, he went directly to see Horpach. The latter was already familiar with the situation, thanks to the TV transmission and the reports of the groups that had returned earlier, bringing with them several hundred photographs. Despite himself, Rohan felt relieved that he didn't have to relate what he had seen to the commander.

Horpach gazed at him intently as he rose from a table on which photographic prints lay scattered across a map of the region. They were both in the main navigation cabin.

"Get a grip, Mr. Rohan," he said. "I understand what you're going through, but more than anything else we need sound judgment. And composure. We have to get to the bottom of this crazy story."

"They had every possible means of protection: energobots, lasers, cannon. The AMC was standing right by the ship. They had the same things that we do," said Rohan in a toneless voice. He sat down abruptly. "I'm sorry," he said.

The commander took a bottle of brandy from a wall cabinet. "An old remedy, sometimes it helps. Have some, Mr. Rohan. In the old days they used this on the battlefield." Rohan swallowed the burning liquid in silence.

"I checked the gauges on all the power units," he said in a tone that sounded like a complaint. "They weren't attacked by anything. They didn't fire a single shot. They just—they just—"

"Went mad?" suggested the commander evenly.

"I'd like to be certain of at least that much. But how could it be? How could that have happened?"

"Did you see the ship's log?"

"No. Gaarb took it. You have it?"

"Yes. After the date of the landing there are only four entries. They're about the ruins you explored. And . . . the 'flies.'"

"I don't follow. What flies?"

"That I don't know. To be precise, it reads as follows." He took the open book from the table. "'No signs of life on the land. Atmospheric composition—' here there are the results of their analyses ... Ah, here it is. 'At 18.40 the second caterpillar patrol returning from the ruins found itself in a local sandstorm with heavy atmospheric discharges. Radio contact was established despite interference. The patrol reports the discovery of significant numbers of small flies covering—'"

The commander stopped and set the book down.

"What comes next? Why aren't you reading to the end?"

"Well, in fact that is the ending. That's where the last entry breaks off."

"There's nothing more?"

"Take a look at the rest yourself."

He pushed the open book over to Rohan. It was covered in illegible scribbles. Rohan stared wide-eyed at the jumble of crisscross lines.

"This looks like a letter b," he said quietly.

"Right. And here there's a G. A capital G. Exactly like it was being written by a small child. Don't you think?"

Rohan said nothing, the empty glass still in his hand. He'd forgotten to put it down. He thought about his ambition of not long ago: He had dreamed of commanding the *Invincible* himself. Now he was grateful to fate that he wasn't the one having to decide about the future of the expedition.

"Go summon all the heads of the specialist groups. Mr. Rohan! Wake up!"

"I'm sorry. A council, commander?"

"That's right. Have them all come to the library."

Fifteen minutes later everyone was already seated in the large square-shaped cabin with colored enamel walls that concealed books and microfilms. The most awful thing of all may well have been the uncanny similarity between the cabins on the *Condor* and the *Invincible*. It was understandable, they were sister ships. But whatever corner Rohan found himself staring into, he couldn't suppress the images of frenzy that had been seared into his memory.

Everyone had their assigned place. Biologist, physician, planetologist, electronic engineers and communications engineers, cyberneticists and physicists—all sat in a half-circle of chairs. These nineteen men constituted the strategic brain of the ship. The captain stood alone by a white screen that had been half lowered.

"Is everyone here familiar with the situation found on board the *Condor?*"

There was a murmured yes from many voices.

"Up till now," said Horpach, "the teams working within the *Condor's* perimeter have recovered twenty-nine bodies. On the ship itself thirty-four have been found, including one that was perfectly preserved after having been frozen in the hibernation chamber. Dr. Nygren, who just returned from there, will give us an overview."

"I don't have a lot to relate," said the diminutive doctor. He walked slowly up to the captain. He was a head shorter than him.

"We found only nine mummified bodies. That is, aside from the one the commander mentioned, which will be examined separately. Most of the remains are really just skeletons or parts of skeletons that we dug out of the sand. The mummification occurred inside the ship, where the conditions were right for it: very low humidity, an almost total absence of saprogenic bacteria, and rather low temperatures. The bodies found out in the open had been subject to decomposition that was accelerated by periods of rain, as the sand here contains a sizeable percentage of iron oxides and iron sulphides that react with weak acids.

Though actually I don't think these details are particularly important. If an exact account of the reactions were needed, we could hand the matter over to our chemist colleagues. In any case, in the conditions outside the ship mummification was all the more impossible since there was a combination of water and other substances it contained, along with the action of the sand over many years. This last factor explains the polished surfaces of the bones."

"Excuse me, doctor," the commander broke in. "The most important thing at the present moment is the cause of decease of these people."

"There were no signs of violent death, at least on the best preserved bodies," the physician stated immediately. He was not looking at anyone; he seemed to be studying something unseen in a hand raised toward his face. "The whole picture suggests that they died of natural causes."

"Meaning?"

"Without any violent operation from outside. Some of the long bones found in isolation are broken, but this kind of damage could have occurred later. It would take more extensive tests to know for sure. On those who were wearing clothing, both the outer skin and the skeleton are unharmed. There are no wounds, aside from small scratches that certainly could not have been the cause of death."

"Then how did they die?"

"That I can't say. One might think it was from hunger or thirst ..."

"There were plentiful reserves of water and foodstuffs," Gaarb remarked from his place.

"I'm aware of that."

For a moment there was silence.

"Mummification is above all a process whereby the organism is deprived of water," explained Nygren. He was still not looking at anyone in the cabin. "The adipose tissues undergo changes, but these can be identified. The thing is ... these people had virtually no such tissues at all. Exactly as if from an extensive period of starvation."

"But not the body preserved in the hibernation chamber," put in Rohan, who was standing behind the back row of seats.

"That's true. But he probably froze to death. He must have gotten into the hibernation chamber somehow or other. He may simply have fallen asleep as his body temperature dropped."

"Is it possible there was a large-scale poisoning?" asked Horpach.

"No."

"Surely you can't be so categorical, doctor."

"I can say this for certain," replied the physician. "In planetary conditions, poisoning can take place either through the lungs, by breathing in gases, or through the alimentary tract, or through the skin. One of the best preserved bodies was wearing breathing equipment. The tank still contained enough oxygen to last for ten or fifteen hours ..."

That's right, thought Rohan to himself. He remembered the man, the shrunken skin on his skull and the traces of discolored marks on his cheeks; and the eye-sockets, from which sand was spilling out.

"These people could not have eaten anything toxic, because there isn't anything to eat at all in this place. On the land, that is. They didn't attempt to take anything from the ocean. The catastrophe occurred soon after they landed. They only sent a single patrol into the heart of the ruins. That was all. A propos, I see McMinn is coming. Dr. McMinn, are you done?"

"I am," said the biochemist from the doorway. All heads turned in his direction. He passed between the chairs and stood next to Nygren. He was still wearing a long laboratory apron.

"You've conducted the analyses?"

"Yes I have."

"Dr. McMinn was examining the body of the man found in the hibernation chamber," explained Nygren. "Can you tell us right away what you found?"

"Nothing," said McMinn. His hair was so light it was impossible to say whether it was simply gray; he had eyes of the same color. Even his eyelids were covered with large freckles. But now his long, horselike face amused no one.

"There was no organic or non-organic poisoning. There was no pathology in any of the enzymatic compounds in the tissues. Blood was normal. The stomach contained the remains of digested hard tack and concentrate."

"Then how did he die?" asked Horpach. He was just as calm as before.

"He simply froze to death," replied McMinn. Only now did he notice he was still wearing his apron. He unclasped it and dropped it onto a nearby empty chair. The slippery material slid off the seat onto the floor.

"So what is your opinion, gentlemen?" asked the unyielding commander.

"I don't have one," said McMinn. "I can only tell you that these people did not die of poisoning."

"Perhaps some kind of rapidly decaying radioactive substance? Or hard radiation?"

"Hard radiation in lethal doses leaves signs: extravasation, petechiae, changes in the makeup of the blood. There were no such changes. And there is no radioactive substance that would disappear without a trace after being ingested eight years ago in a lethal dose. The levels of radioactivity here are lower than on Earth. These men did not encounter any form of radioactivity. That I can guarantee."

"But something killed them!" said the planetologist Ballmin, raising his voice.

McMinn was silent. Nygren murmured something to him. The biochemist nodded and walked out past the rows of seated scientists. At that point Nygren also stepped away from the dais and took his place.

"The matter does not look good," said the commander. "In any case, we can't expect any help from the biologists. Do any of you gentlemen have anything to say?"

"I do."

Sarner, an atomic physicist, stood up.

"The explanation of the *Condor*'s end lies in the ship itself," he said. He looked at each of them in turn with eyes like those of a far-seeing hawk. His black hair contrasted with irises that were almost white.

"What I mean is, the answer is there, we just don't yet know how to read it. The disorder in the cabins, the untouched supplies, the arrangement and location of the corpses, the damage to the equipment—all this means something."

"If you have nothing else to say—" Gaarb interjected in a disappointed voice.

"Just a minute. We find ourselves in darkness. We need to look for a path. For the moment we know very little. I have a feeling that we saw certain things on board the *Condor* that we've been afraid to mention. That's why we keep returning so stubbornly to the hypothesis of poisoning and the collective delirium it supposedly gave rise to. In our own best interests, though also out of consideration for those people, we have to be ruthless with regard to the facts. I would ask, or rather, I would categorically move, that each of you here and now say what you found to be the most shocking thing on the *Condor*. Something you may not have shared with anyone. That you told yourself needs to be forgotten."

Sarner took his seat. After briefly wrestling with himself, Rohan spoke of the pieces of soap he had found in the bathroom.

Then Gralev stood up. Under their covering of torn maps and books, the decks were strewn with dried excrement.

Someone else mentioned a can of food that bore toothmarks, as if someone had tried to gnaw it open. Gaarb had been most horrified by the scrawls in the ship's log, and the word "flies." He did not stop there.

"Let's say a wave of poisonous gases emerged from the tectonic gap in the 'city,' and the wind carried it to the rocket. If the hatch happened to have been left open by mistake—"

"Only the outside hatch was slightly open, Dr. Gaarb. The sand in the airlock showed that clearly. The interior hatchway was closed."

"They might have closed it later, after they began to feel the effects of the gas."

"Come on, Dr. Gaarb, that's not possible. You can't open the inner hatch when the outer one is open. They only open in sequence, to prevent any possibility of carelessness or lack of caution."

"But one thing is certain in my mind—that the thing happened suddenly. Mass madness—I won't even mention that there are cases of psychosis during space flights, but never on a planet's surface, especially within a few hours of landing. Mass madness affecting the entire crew can only have been the result of poisoning."

"Or reversion to infancy," put in Sarner.

"What? What are you talking about?" said Gaarb, taken aback. "Is that supposed to be a joke?"

"I wouldn't joke in a situation like this. I mention reversion to infancy because no one else has brought it up. And yet—the scribbles in the logbook, the torn-up star catalogues, the letters formed with such difficulty . . . You all saw them, right?"

"But what does that mean?" asked Nygren. "Are you saying it's a recognized disorder?"

"No. I don't believe it is one, am I right, doctor?"

"Definitely not."

There was another silence. The commander hesitated.

"This could lead us up the garden path. Necroptic soundings are never conclusive. But at the present moment I don't know what further harm it could do. Dr. Sax . . ."

The neurophysiologist showed the image obtained from the brain of the man found frozen to death in the hibernation chamber; he also made a point of mentioning the syllables that had remained in the dead man's auditory memory. This gave rise to a veritable barrage of questions; Rohan found himself caught in the crossfire, as he had also taken part in the experiment. But it didn't lead to any conclusions.

"These spots put me in mind of the 'flies,'" said Gaarb. "Wait a minute. What if there were different causes of death? Let's say the crew fell victim to some kind of poisonous insects—after all, small bite marks cannot be detected on mummified skin. While the man in the hibernation chamber was simply trying to escape from the insects and avoid the fate of his fellow crew members . . . and he froze to death."

"But why was he struck with amnesia before he died?"

"Loss of memory, you mean? Has that been established beyond a doubt?"

"Inasmuch as the results of the necroptic scan can be trusted."

"But what do you think of the insect hypothesis?"

"Dr. Lauda should say what he thinks."

Lauda was the ship's Chief Paleobiologist. He rose to his feet and waited for everyone to settle down.

"It's not by accident that we haven't said a word about the so-called flies. Anyone who has the slightest notion of biology is aware that no organism can live outside of its defined biotope, which is to say, the primary unit consisting of its habitat and all the species living in it. This is how things are in all of known space. Life either produces a huge variety of forms, or does not arise at all. Insects could not have come into being without the simultaneous development of ground-dwelling plants, other symmetrical invertebrate organisms, and so on. I'm not going to set forth the general theory of evolution, I think it's enough for me to assure you that this is not possible. Here there are no poisonous flies, or any other arthropods, hymenoptera, arachnids. Nor any forms related to them."

"How can you be so certain?" exclaimed Ballmin.

"If you were a student of mine, Dr. Ballmin, you wouldn't have been accepted on board because you'd have failed your exam," returned the paleobiologist unruffled, and the others smiled involuntarily. "I don't know how you'd have done in paleontology, but in evolutionary biology you'd have gotten an F!"

"This is turning into the usual disagreement among specialists—isn't it all a waste of time?" someone whispered to Rohan from behind. Rohan turned around and saw Jarg's broad sunburned face; the latter gave him a conspiratorial wink.

"Well, maybe the flies aren't from here," said Ballmin, not giving up. "Maybe they were brought here from somewhere else."

"Where?"

"From a planet affected by a nova."

Everyone began to speak at once. It took a good moment for all those present to quieten down again.

"Gentlemen!" said Sarner. "I know where Dr. Ballmin got his notion. From Dr. Gralev."

"What can I say? I won't deny it," put in the physicist.

"Very well. Let's agree that we can no longer afford the luxury of plausible hypotheses. That what we need are crazy ones. So be it. Let's ask the biologists: Say a ship from a nova-affected planet were to have brought insects from home. Could they have adapted to local conditions?"

"If the hypothesis is supposed to be crazy, then yes, they could have," agreed Lauda from his place. "But even a crazy hypothesis has to account for everything."

"Meaning?"

"Meaning that it'll have to explain what disfigured the entire exterior hull of the *Condor*, to the point that, as the engineers tell me, the ship needs extensive repairs in order to even be flightworthy. Do you really believe that insects could have adapted to the point of eating molybdenum alloy? It's one of the hardest substances in the universe. Engineer Petersen, what could have damaged the plating?"

"If it was properly riveted, then basically nothing," replied the Second Engineer. "It could be partially drilled into with diamonds, but you'd need huge numbers of bits and a thousand hours. Acid would be quicker. But you're talking about inorganic acids that have to be applied at temperatures of at least two thousand degrees, with the use of the necessary catalysts."

"Then what in your view caused the damage to the *Condor*?"

"I have no idea. It would look that way if it sat in a bath of acid at the requisite temperature. But how it got that way without plasma torches or catalysts, I can't even imagine."

"So much for your 'flies,' Dr. Ballmin," said Lauda, and sat down.

"I don't see any point in continuing the discussion," put in the commander, who till now had been silent. "Perhaps it was too soon for it. There's nothing left to do but carry out tests. We'll divide into three teams. One team will take the ruins, the second the *Condor*, and the third will make a series of expeditions into the Western Desert. That's all we can manage, since even if we get some of the *Condor*'s vehicles working, I can't remove more than fourteen energobots from the perimeter, and degree three will continue to be in force."

THE FIRST

A slick, smoldering blackness surrounded him on all sides. He was choking. With helpless movements he tried to push back the seemingly immaterial coils that wound around him, engulfing him more and more; with a cry stuck in his swollen throat he looked in vain for a weapon; he was naked; he gathered all his strength for one final shout. A deafening noise tore him from his sleep. Rohan jumped out of his bunk barely conscious, knowing only that he was plunged in a darkness in which the alarm signal was repeatedly sounding. This was no longer the nightmare. He turned on the light, climbed into his jump suit, and ran to the elevator. People were crowded around it on every deck. The insistent noise of the signal could be heard, red ALARM signs flashed on the walls. He ran onto the bridge. The commander, dressed as he had been during the day, stood before the main monitor.

"I've already called off the alarm," he said calmly. "It was just rain. But take a look, Mr. Rohan—it's quite a spectacle."

Indeed, the screen, which showed the upper part of the night sky, was bright with innumerable sparks from electrical discharges. Drops of rain falling from the sky struck against the invisible dome-shaped force field shielding the *Invincible* and, instantly becoming microscopic flaming explosions, lit up the entire landscape with a coruscating glow like the northern lights magnified a hundred times.

"The automatons should be better programmed," said Rohan softly, fully awake by now. Sleep had left him. "I should tell Terner not to turn on the annihilator. Otherwise the slightest handful of sand brought by the wind is going to wake us up in the middle of the night."

"Let's just say it was a drill. A dry run," replied the commander, who seemed to be in an unexpectedly good mood. "It's four o'clock. You can go back to your cabin, Mr. Rohan."

"To be honest, I don't feel like it. Would you ...?"

"I slept already. I only need four hours. After sixteen years in space a person's rhythm of sleep and waking bears no relation to his terrestrial habits. I was thinking about how to provide the best protection for the expeditionary teams. It's rather cumbersome, trailing around everywhere with the energobots and setting up force fields. What do you think about it?"

"Each man could be given an individual transmitter. But that's not a perfect solution either. A person in a force field bubble can't touch anything—you know how it is. And if the radius of the field is reduced too far, you can burn yourself. I've seen it happen."

"I even weighed the option of not letting anyone out onto the land, and using robots to do the work, by remote control," admitted the commander. "But that would only do for a few hours, a day, whereas it looks like we could be staying here longer ..."

"So what do you mean to do?"

"Each team will have a base camp protected by a force field, but individual researchers have to have full freedom of movement. Otherwise we'll be so well protected from accidents that we'll never accomplish anything. The one essential condition is that any individual working outside the force field is backed up by someone who *is* protected, to watch over his movements. Stay within view—that's the most important rule on Regis III."

"Where am I going to be assigned?"

"Would you like to work at the *Condor*?—I see the answer is no. All right. Then it's either the city or the desert. Your choice."

"I'll opt for the city, captain. I still have the feeling that that's where the secret lies."

"Possibly. Very well, so tomorrow, or actually today, as it's almost daybreak, you'll take the same team you had yesterday. I'll give you a couple more arctans. It'd be a good idea to take a couple of hand-held lasers too, because I have the sense that 'it' operates at short distance ..."

"What does?"

"I wish I knew. Oh—you should also take a field kitchen, so you're completely independent of us, and if necessary you can work without permanent material contact with the ship ..."

★

The red sun, which gave almost no heat, had dropped over the horizon. The shadows of the grotesque structures lengthened and joined together. The wind constantly shifted the dunes that lay among the metal pyramids. Rohan was sitting on the top of a heavy transporter, gazing through a telescope at Gralev and Chen, who were outside the force field, plodding along at the base of a blackish honeycomb. The strap of the light-ray gun was chafing the nape of his neck. He shifted it back as far as it would go, without taking his eyes off the other two men.

The plasma torch Chen was holding shone like a tiny, blinding diamond. From inside the vehicle he could hear the recurring rhythm of a call signal, but he didn't turn his head even for a moment. He heard the driver responding to the base.

"Sir! The commander is ordering us back to the ship immediately!" shouted Jarg in an animated voice, sticking his head through the turret hatch.

"Back to the ship? What for?"

"I don't know. They keep repeating the signal for immediate return, and four times the EV."

"The EV? Ouch, I've gotten stiff. That means we need to get a move on. Give me the microphone, and get the flares out."

Within ten minutes everyone who had been outside the force field was in the vehicles. Rohan led his small convoy at the greatest speed the hilly terrain permitted. Blank, who was now serving as communications officer, suddenly passed him the headphones. Rohan lowered himself into the metal interior of the transporter that smelled of heated plastic, and as the air blowing from the A/C unit mussed up his hair, listened in to the exchange of messages between the *Invincible* and Gallagher's team working in the western desert. A storm seemed to be brewing. From early morning the barometers had been indicating low air pressure, but it was only now that level, dark blue clouds appeared over the horizon. The sky above them was clear. Interference was plentiful—there was so much crackling in the headphones that they had to communicate in Morse code. Rohan heard a series of standard signals. He had tuned in too late and couldn't figure out what it was about. All he understood was that Gallagher's team was also returning to base as fast as they could, while the ship itself was on high alert and all the physicians were standing by.

"Physicians at the ready," he said to Ballmin and Gralev, who were looking at him waiting for an explanation. "There must have been an accident. But it can't have been anything serious. Maybe a landslide, someone got trapped ..."

He said this because everyone knew Gallagher's men had been assigned to carry out geological excavations in a location determined by a preliminary recon party. But the truth was that he himself didn't believe it was just a regular work accident. They were only about three and a half miles from base, but the other team had evidently been summoned back quite a lot earlier, because at the moment they saw the dark vertical shape of the *Invincible* they crossed a completely fresh set of caterpillar tracks, which in this wind would not have remained visible for more than half an hour.

They came up to the perimeter of the outer force field and began calling the bridge to be allowed in. They had to wait a strangely long time before receiving a response. Finally the usual blue lights came on and they drove through. The team from the *Condor* was already there. So they were the ones who'd been brought back first, not Gallagher's team. Some transporters had pulled up by the ramp, others blocked the approach; confusion reigned, people were running around, sinking to their knees in sand, while the automatons shone flashlights every which way.

Dusk was already falling. For a moment Rohan couldn't figure out what was going on in all the commotion. All at once, a beam of blinding white exploded on the scene. The huge searchlight made the rocket look like a gigantic lighthouse. Far off in the desert it picked out a column of rocking lights that moved up, down, and sideways, as if an actual armada of ships was approaching. Once again the lights came on to indicate an opening in the force field. Before the vehicles even came to a complete standstill, the men of Gallagher's team started jumping down onto the sand. A second searchlight was being wheeled from the ramp, and between the crowded lines of vehicles that had been moved aside, a group of people accompanied a stretcher on which someone was lying.

At the moment the stretcher passed by, Rohan pushed past those standing in front of him and was struck dumb. In the first instant he thought there actually had been an accident, but the arms and legs of the man on the stretcher were tied down.

His whole body straining so hard that the ropes he was restrained with were creaking, he was whimpering in the most ghastly manner, his mouth wide open. The group moved off, guided by a bright circle from the searchlights that led the way, while Rohan stood in the darkness, his ears still ringing with that inhuman yelping sound, unlike anything he had ever heard before. The white patch of light and the little figures moving inside it receded, ascended the ramp, and disappeared into the broad opening of the freight hatch. Rohan started asking around about what had happened, but the people nearby were all from the *Condor* team and knew no more than he did.

It was some time before he recovered enough to bring some order to the place. The line of vehicles that had been held up now moved up the ramp in a roar of engines; the lights over the elevator came on, the crowd standing at its base thinned out. Rohan was one of the last to ride up, along with the heavily laden arctans, whose tranquility seemed to him a particularly cruel mockery. Inside the rocket the PA system and the intercom sounded constantly; the alarm signals summoning the doctors were still lit up, though they were soon turned off. The place emptied out a little. Some of the crew had gone down to the mess; he heard conversations in a passageway filled with the sound of footsteps; a straggling arctan trod heavily by on the way to the robot hold. Finally everyone had dispersed, while he stood there alone, overcome by inertia, as if he'd lost hope of understanding what had happened, as if overwhelmed by the certainty that there would not be, could not be, any explanation.

"Rohan!"

He started. Gaarb was standing in front of him. The exclamation sobered him up.

"Oh, it's you. Did you ... did you see, doctor? Who was it?"

"Kertelen."

"What? No way."

"I saw him almost up till the very end."

"The end of what?"

"I was with him," said Gaarb in a unnaturally quiet tone of voice. Rohan saw the lights of the passageway reflected in his eyeglasses.

"The exploratory team sent into the desert ... ," he mumbled.

"Right."

"What happened to him?"

"Gallagher had identified the location based on seismological soundings. We found ourselves in a labyrinth of small, winding ravines," Gaarb said slowly, as if he were not speaking to Rohan so much as trying to recall for himself the sequence of events. "There are soft cliffs there of organic origin that have been hollowed out by water; there are any number of caves, potholes; we had to leave the caterpillars behind. We kept close together, there were eleven of us. The ferrometers were indicating significant quantities of iron in the vicinity; we were looking for it. Kertelen thought there must be some kind of machinery hidden someplace ..."

"Right, he said something to me along those lines. What then?"

"In one of the caves, close to the entrance—under the mud there were even stalactites and stalagmites—he found something like an automaton."

"No kidding!"

"It's not what you think. It was nothing but a corpse, it had been consumed, eaten away, not by rust because it was made of some kind of rustproof alloy, but it was corroded, rotten. It was just remnants."

"But maybe there are others ..."

"The thing is, the automaton was at least three hundred thousand years old ..."

"How do you know?"

"Because limestone had formed on its upper surface as the water dripping from the stalactites evaporated. Gallagher himself did the calculations, according to the rate of evaporation, way the deposit was formed, and its thickness. Three hundred thousand years is the most conservative estimate. Besides, you know what the automaton actually resembled? The ruins!"

"So it wasn't really an automaton."

"No, it must have been able to move, but not on two feet. And not in a crablike way. Though we didn't have time to examine it, because right afterwards ..."

"What happened?"

"Every so often I counted the men. I was protected by a force field, I had to watch over them, you understand? But everyone was wearing masks, you know how it is, everyone looks the same, and their suits could no longer be told apart by color, they were all covered with mud. At a certain point I was one man short. I called everyone together and we started searching.

Kertelen had been delighted at his discovery, and he was poking around looking for more ... I thought he'd simply wandered into some branch of the ravine—there were lots of side gullies there, though they were all short, shallow, well lit ... All of a sudden he appeared from behind a bend. He was already in that state. Nygren was with us, he thought it was heat stroke ..."

"So what is actually wrong with him?"

"He's unconscious. Though in fact that's not true. He can walk, move, it's just that you can't communicate with him. Also, he's lost the ability to talk. You heard his voice?"

"Yes."

"He seems to be flagging now. Before, it was even worse. He didn't recognize any of us. In the first instant that was the most terrible thing. I called out, 'Kertelen, where've you been?', but he walked by me as if he was deaf, he passed among us and went up the ravine, and the way he was moving gave everyone the chills. It was like it wasn't him, you know. He didn't react to being called, so we had to run after him. The things that happened then! In a word he had to be tied up, otherwise we'd not have been able to bring him back."

"What do the doctors say?"

"As usual, they're talking Latin, but aside from that they know nothing. Nygren and Sax are with the commander, you can go ask them."

Gaarb moved off with a heavy step, his head tilting the way it always did. Rohan got in the elevator and went up to the bridge. It was deserted, but as he passed the cartographic cabins he heard Sax's voice through a partly open door. He went in.

"It's as if the memory has been completely obliterated. That's how it looks," the neurophysiologist was saying. He was standing with his back to Rohan, examining an X-ray he held in his hands. The commander was at a desk, the open log book in front of him, his arm raised and resting on shelves of tightly rolled star maps. He was listening in silence to Sax as the latter slowly slid the X-ray into an envelope.

"Amnesia. But of a highly unusual kind. He's lost not only the memory of who he is, but also his speech, the ability to write and read. The fact is, it's more than amnesia: It's an utter collapse, an annihilation of the personality. Nothing is left but the most primitive actions. He can walk and eat, though only when food is put into his mouth. He can take hold of things, but ..."

"Can he hear and see?"

"Yes. For sure. But he doesn't understand what he's seeing. He can't tell people from objects."

"Reflexes?"

"Within the norm. That's a central matter."

"Central?"

"Controlled from the central nervous system. It's like all traces of memory were completely erased in one go."

"So the man from the *Condor* ..."

"Yes. I'm certain of it. That was the same thing."

"I saw something like this once before," the commander said ever so quietly, almost in a whisper. His eyes were on Rohan, but his mind was elsewhere. "It was in space ..."

"Yes! Why didn't I think of that!" exclaimed the neurophysiologist. "Amnesia after a magnetic stroke, right?"

"That's right."

"I've never see a case of it. I only know the phenomenon from theory. It happened a long time ago, during a high-velocity passage through powerful magnetic fields, yes?"

"Yes. That is to say, in very particular circumstances. The intensity of the field isn't so important as its gradient and the suddenness of the change. Where large gradients exist in space—and some of them are dramatic—the sensors detect them from far off. Back in the day there were no sensors ..."

"That's true," confirmed the physician. "That's true ... Ammerhatten conducted experiments like that on cats and dogs. He exposed them to massive magnetic fields, till they lost their memory."

"Yes, it has something to do with electrical stimulation of the brain."

"But in this case," Sax wondered aloud, "along with Gaarb's report we have statements from all of his men. A powerful magnetic field ... I mean, it would need to be hundreds of thousands of gauss, wouldn't it?"

"Hundreds of thousands wouldn't be enough. It would have to be millions," the commander said brusquely. It was only now that he actually looked at Rohan.

"Come in and close the door, Mr. Rohan."

"Millions? Wouldn't the onboard equipment pick up a field that big?"

"Not necessarily," replied Horpach. "If it were concentrated in a very small area—if, let's say, it had the dimensions of this globe—and if it were screened on the outside ..."

"In a word, if Kertelen had put his head between the poles of a gigantic electromagnet ... ?"

"Even that would not be sufficient. The field would have to oscillate at the requisite frequency."

"But there weren't any magnets there, nor any machinery except for that rusting scrap. Nothing but rainwashed ravines, gravel, and sand."

"And the caves," added Horpach softly, as if by the by.

"And the caves ... Do you think someone might have pulled him into one of the caves, that there was a magnet there—no, surely that would be ..."

"Then how do you explain it?" asked the commander, as if discouraged and wearied by the conversation. The physician said nothing.

At 3.40 a.m. all the decks of the *Invincible* were filled with the continual ringing of the alarm signal. People leaped out of bed cursing left, right and center, threw their clothes on and rushed to their stations. Rohan found himself on the bridge five minutes after the bells first sounded. The commander had not yet arrived. Rohan hurried to the main monitor. To the east, the black night was lit up by a multitude of white flashes. It was as though the rocket were being attacked by a meteor shower from a single radiant. He checked the controls of the force field. He'd programmed the automatons himself, so they couldn't be reacting to rain or to a sandstorm. Something flew out of the unseen dark of the desert and burst in a string of fiery fragments; the discharges took place on the surface of the force field, where the bizarre projectiles, bouncing off in flames, made parabolic trails of fading light, or slid down the convex exterior of the field. The tops of the dunes leaped out of the gloom for an instant then vanished again, the needles of the dials twitched idly—the actual force used by the Dirac cannons to destroy the mysterious bombardment was relatively low. Hearing the commander's steps behind him, Rohan glanced at the array of spectroscopic sensors.

"Nickel, iron, manganese, beryllium, titanium," Horpach read from the lighted screen as he stood next to Rohan. "What I wouldn't give to see exactly what this is."

"A rain of metal particles," Rohan said slowly. "Judging from the discharges, they must be small ..."

"I wouldn't mind a closer look," murmured the captain. "What do you think, Mr. Rohan—shall we risk it?"

"Turning off the force field?"

"Yes. Just for a split second. A small amount of them will find their way into the perimeter, then we turn the field back on and shut out the rest."

For a long moment Rohan didn't reply.

"I suppose we could," he said at last, hesitantly. But before the commander could go up to the main console, the profusion of lights faded as quickly as it had appeared, to be replaced with the kind of darkness known only to moonless planets orbiting far from the Galaxy's central concentrations of stars.

"No catch tonight," Horpach said softly. He stood for a long while with his hand on the main shut-off lever, then, with a slight nod to Rohan, he left. The whine of the signal calling off the alarm sounded throughout the ship. Rohan sighed, took one last look at the blackness filling the monitors, and went off to sleep.

THE CLOUD

They were already growing accustomed to the planet—to its unchanging desert surface with faint shadows of clouds that always seemed on the point of melting away and were unnaturally light in color, the stars often shining behind them even during the day. To the hiss of sand blowing underfoot and beneath the wheels of the vehicles; to the red, ponderous sun, whose touch was incomparably more delicate than on Earth, such that when you presented your back to it, instead of warmth you felt merely a kind of silent presence. In the morning the teams rode out to their respective destinations; the energobots disappeared among the dunes, rocking like clumsy boats; the dust settled, and those remaining behind on the *Invincible* discussed what they'd be having for dinner, or what the radar bosun said today to the communications officer, or they strove to remember the name of the pilot who'd lost his leg six years ago in an accident on the Terra 5 navigational satellite. This was what they talked about as they sat around on empty canisters under the hull, whose shadow, like the gnomon of an immense sundial, rotated as it lengthened till it touched the line of energobots. From that moment they would stand up and begin to look out for the returning teams. The latter in turn, when they appeared hungry and tired, suddenly lost all the vigor generated by their work in the metallic ruins of the city, and after a week even the team from the *Condor* stopped bringing back sensational news that boiled down to the fact they'd managed to identify a particular person among the remains in that place. What they recovered from there, which in the first few days had been marked with terror, was packed away tidily (for how else could one speak of the methodical process of arranging all the surviving human remains in hermetic containers that then were stowed away in the hold), and vanished from view.

At such times, instead of the relief that might be expected, the people who continued to sift through the sand around the *Condor*'s stern and to rummage through its interior began to experience a sort of tedium, as if they'd forgotten what happened to its crew and were occupying themselves with the collecting of idiotic trifles that had belonged to no one knew who in distant times, and had been left behind by their long-gone owners. Thus, in the absence of documents that might explain the mystery, instead they came back with an old harmonica or a tangram, and these objects, stripped of their uncanny, mystical origins, went the rounds, becoming as it were the communal property of the crew. Rohan, who before would never have believed such a thing possible, within a week was behaving exactly like all the others. It was only sometimes when he was alone that he asked himself what he was actually doing here; at such moments he felt that all their work—all that eager bustling about, the complicated process of tests, x-rays, samples, geological drilling, all of which was complicated by the permanent need to maintain degree three, with the opening and closing of force fields, the aiming of the lasers, whose field of fire was finely calculated, with continuous visual oversight, endless counting, communication on multiple channels—that all of this was just a massive self-deception. That when it came down to it they were simply waiting for another accident, some new misfortune, and were only pretending that this was not the case. To begin with, people would gather each morning outside the sick bay of the *Invincible* to get an update on Kertelen's condition. In their eyes, he was not so much the victim of a bizarre attack as an inhuman creature, a being different from all of the rest of them; it was quite as if they'd begun believing in fairy tales and thought it was possible for a human, one of their own kind, to be transformed by the alien, hostile forces of the planet into a monster. In reality he was nothing more than a cripple; actually it turned out that his mind, bare as that of a new-born baby, was capable of learning from his doctors, and he was gradually acquiring speech, exactly like a small baby in fact. The sick bay no longer resounded with the whimpering noise that was unlike any human sound, and was terrible because the senseless babble of a child was coming from the throat of a grown man. Within a week Kertelen started to utter his first syllables and already recognized the physicians, though he could not pronounce their names.

Then, with the beginning of the second week, interest in his person diminished all the more when the doctors explained that he would not be able to say anything about the circumstances of the accident, even if he were to recover his normal state, or rather, complete his unusual though essential education.

In the meantime, the work took its own course. Maps of the city and details of the structure of its bushy pyramids were amassed, though the purpose for which they had been built remained unclear. The commander concluded that further examination of the *Condor* was unlikely to produce anything new, and he halted it. The ship itself had to be abandoned, because the repairs needed on the hull were beyond the capabilities of the engineers, especially when there were so many more pressing matters to attend to. All they did was transfer a large number of energobots, transporters, jeeps, and equipment to the *Invincible*, while the wreck itself—for it was in effect a wreck after being so thoroughly emptied out—was closed up; they consoled themselves with the thought that either they or the next expedition to visit would eventually bring the cruiser back to its home port. Horpach then sent the team from the *Condor* to the north; under Regnar's leadership it joined up with Gallagher's team. Rohan was now the coordinator of all the exploratory work; he only left the vicinity of the *Invincible* for short periods, and that not every day.

In the network of ravines channeled out by underground springs, both groups made curious discoveries.

The strata of sedimentary rock were interspersed with layers of a ruddy-black substance that was of non-geological, non-planetary origin. The specialists were not able to say much more about it. It looked as if on the base of an old basalt shield, the bottom level of the crust, millions of years ago a huge number of metallic fragments had been deposited—perhaps they were metal shards (someone suggested the hypothesis that a gigantic nickel-iron meteor had exploded in Regis's atmosphere and, coming down in a burning rain, had fused with the rock of that ancient time) which, subject to gradual oxidation and entering into chemical reactions with the environment, had eventually turned into seams of sediment that were brownish-black, in places dark crimson in color.

The drillings so far had barely touched on a small part of the seams in the terrain, whose geological complexity was enough to make the head of even the most experienced planetologist spin. When a bore was drilled all the way down to the basalt from a billion years ago, it transpired that the rock superimposed upon it, despite a well advanced recrystalization, contained organic carbon. To begin with it was thought that this was a former ocean bed. But in the seams that were already mineral coal they found fossils of numerous plant species that could only grow in dry conditions. By degrees the catalogue of the planet's continental life forms filled out. It was already known that three hundred million years ago primitive reptilians had prowled its jungles. The remains of the spinal column and horny jaw of one of them were brought back by the scientists with a sense of triumph that the crew did not share. Evolution appeared to have taken place on land two times. The first twilight of the living world came around a hundred million years ago; at that time, plants and animals died out abruptly, in all probability as a result of a nearby nova. Life picked up again afterwards, however, and flourished in new forms; true, neither the number nor the condition of the evidence they found permitted a more exact classification. The planet had never produced any mammal-like forms. Ninety million years later another star exploded, though this time a long way away; it could be detected in the form of elementary isotopes. According to approximate calculations, the hard radiation was not so intense on the surface as to reap a massive harvest of victims. Such a fact made it all the more unaccountable that from that time, plant and animal traces occurred less and less frequently in the more recent strata. On the other hand, there were increasing quantities of compressed "loam" containing antimonite, molybdenum oxide, ferrous oxides, and salts of nickel, cobalt, and titanium.

These metallic layers, dating from between eight and six million years ago, and relatively shallow, contained in places strong centers of radioactivity, but on the scale of the planet's existence it was radiation of relatively short duration. It was as if in that time something had brought about a series of violent but localized nuclear reactions, the results of which had been preserved in the metallic sediment. In addition to the hypothesis of the ferro-radioactive meteor, other entirely fantastical ideas were put forward, linking the curious knots of radioactive intensity to the catastrophe in the Lira planetary system and the annihilation of its civilization. It was suggested that during attempts to colonize Regis III, there were atomic clashes among the ships sent out from the endangered system. This, however, did not explain the dimensions of the curious metallic strata that were also found during test drilling in other remote locations. In any case, a picture emerged that was as puzzling as it was irrefutable: On this planet, life on land had died off in the space of a few million years, at the same time the metal strata began to appear. The destruction of living forms could not have been caused by radioactivity. The overall amount of radiation was calculated in terms of nuclear denotations; it totaled no more than twenty to thirty megatonnes, spread over hundreds of millennia. It was obvious that such explosions (if indeed they were explosions, and not some other kind of nuclear reaction) could not have presented a serious threat to the evolution of biological forms.

Suspecting a connection between the metal strata and the ruins of the city, the scientists insisted on further research. This involved several complications, since the opencast digging required the removal of large masses of earth. The only solution was to drive in an adit; such a thing was problematic since the people working underground were no longer protected by any force field. The eventual decision to continue the work despite everything was spurred by the discovery, at a depth of about seventy feet, in a seam rich in iron oxide, of curiously shaped, rusted remains that resembled the corroded, broken parts of some kind of microscopic mechanisms.

On the nineteenth day after they had landed, in the region where the mining teams were at work there appeared roiling clouds that were denser and darker than anything seen before on the planet. Around midday a storm blew up that far exceeded terrestrial storms in the violence of its electrical discharges. Sky and rocks were joined by a tangle of incessant lightning strikes. The swollen waters, coursing through the twisting ravines, began to submerge the walkways they had dug out. The men had to leave the place and take shelter along with the automatons under the main dome of the force field, which was struck by mile-high bolts of lightning. The storm moved slowly westward, where a black wall crisscrossed with lightning obscured the entire horizon over the ocean. On their way back to the *Invincible* the mining teams found a large number of tiny black metal specks lying on the sand in their path. They were taken to be the infamous "flies." Carefully collected, they were brought to the ship, where the scientists examined them, though there was no question of their being the remains of insects. There was yet another council of specialists, which at several points erupted in heated debate. In the end it was decided to dispatch an expedition to the north-east, beyond the region of the meandering ravines and the seams of iron compounds, since on the caterpillar tracks of the *Condor*'s transporters small quantities of interesting minerals had been discovered that had not been found in the regions explored hitherto.

The next day, under Regnar's command twenty-two men with supplies of oxygen, food, and nuclear fuel set out in a fully equipped convoy that also included energobots, the *Condor's* mobile cannon, transporters, and robots, among which were a dozen arctans carrying automatic excavators and drills. Permanent radio and TV contact was maintained up to the moment where the curvature of the planet impeded the direct line of ultra-short waves. At that point the *Invincible* launched into stationary orbit a television relay, allowing it to continue to have reception. The convoy was on the march the entire day. At night it formed into a defensive circle and protected itself with a force field; the next day it set off again. Around noon Regnar informed Rohan that he was stopping at the foot of some ruins he wished to examine more closely; they were located inside a small, shallow crater and were almost completely covered in sand. An hour later radio reception began to deteriorate due to heavy static interference. The communications technicians shifted to a short-wave band which was clearer. Soon after that, when the rumblings of a distant storm moving to the east, which is to say, in the direction the expedition had taken, began to grow quieter, contact was suddenly interrupted. The loss of reception was preceded by a dozen or more increasingly powerful fadings; the strangest thing, though, was the simultaneous worsening of TV reception, which, being relayed from outside the atmosphere, was not dependent on the condition of the ionosphere. At one o'clock communication broke off completely. None of the technicians, or even the physicists who were summoned to help, could make head or tail of the phenomenon. It looked as though a wall of metal had descended somewhere in the desert, preventing the team now 100 miles away from having contact with the *Invincible*.

Rohan, who had not left the commander's side the entire time, could see how uneasy the latter was. To begin with he himself felt it was groundless. He thought that perhaps the storm cloud moving in the same direction as the expedition had some kind of strange screening action. But when asked if it was possible for ionized air to form such a thick layer, the physicists were doubtful. Around six o'clock the storm died down, yet contact still could not be made. After sending numerous messages to which no response came, Horpach dispatched two reconnaissance craft of the flying saucer type.

One flew a thousand feet or so above the desert, while the other ascended to an altitude of two and a half miles, serving as a TV relay for the first. Rohan, the commander, and Gralev, with a dozen others including Ballmin and Sax, stood at the main monitor on the bridge, directly observing everything that was within the field of vision of the first craft's pilot. Beyond the region of the ravines sunk in deep shadow, the desert opened up with its endless lines of dunes, presently striped with black as the sun dropped toward the west. In the oblique light, which made the landscape look especially lugubrious, the low-flying craft occasionally crossed small craters filled to the brim with sand. Some could be made out only because of a central cone belonging to a volcano extinct for many centuries. The terrain was gradually rising and becoming less monotonous. Tall outcrops of rock rose from the waves of sand, forming into a system of whimsically jagged chains of hills. Solitary pinnacles recalled the hulls of shattered ships, or gigantic human figures. The slopes were gouged by sharp lines of gullies filled with pock-marked cones. Eventually the sands dropped behind for good, giving way to a wasteland of vertiginous cliffs and scattered rubble. Here and there, looking from a distance like rivers, were the zigzag crevasses of tectonic cracks in the planet's crust. The landscape was becoming moonlike; at the same time, TV reception began to get worse, the image trembling and fragmentary. The order was given to increase the strength of the signal, but that only temporarily improved picture quality.

The rocks, which up to this point had been off-white in color, were growing darker and darker. The towering ridges, receding into the distance, took on a brownish hue with a venomous metallic sheen; in places there were patches of velvety blackness, as if the rock there was covered with dense but dead vegetation. All at once, sound came from the previously silent first craft. The pilot shouted that he could hear the automatic positioning transmitters of the expedition's lead vehicle. But the men on the bridge heard only his voice, weak and seemingly fading, as he began to call the Regnar team.

The sun was very low by now. In its blood-red light, ahead of the craft there appeared a black wall, swirling like a cloud, and extending from the surface of the rocks to three thousand feet in the air. Nothing could be seen beyond it. If it hadn't been for the slow, even movement of billowing layers in this mass of black that was in places inky dark, and elsewhere gleamed metallically with a livid crimson, it could have been mistaken for an unusually shaped mountain. The horizontal rays of the sun revealed cavernous openings filled with an inexplicable momentary glitter, as if they were occupied by furious whirling swarms composed of flashing crystals of black ice. At first glance it seemed to the viewers that the cloud was moving toward the flying craft, but this was an optical illusion: The plane was simply approaching the peculiar obstacle at a steady velocity.

"RC 4 to base. Should I rise above the cloud, over," came the muffled voice of the pilot. A split second later the commander responded:

"Number One to RC 4, stop before the cloud!"

"RC 4 to base, stopping," the pilot replied immediately; Rohan thought he heard relief in his voice. By now only a thousand feet separated the craft from the extraordinary formation, which was spreading to both sides as if reaching for the horizon. Now almost the entire monitor was filled with the surface of a gigantic, impossibly vertical sea that looked as if it was made of coal. The plane stopped moving toward it, but all of a sudden, before anyone could say anything, the turgidly undulating mass sent out long streaming offshoots that obscured the picture. At the same time the image faltered, shook, and disappeared in a mesh of dwindling static.

"RC 4! RC 4!" called the radio operator.

"This is RC 8," came the sudden voice of the pilot of the second craft, which till now had merely been used as a relay for the first. "RC 8 to base, shall I give you visual, over!"

"Base to RC 8, give us visual!"

The screen filled with a confusion of spinning black eddies. It was the same picture, but viewed from an height of two and a half miles. The cloud could be seen resting in a long uniform mass against a rising mountain buttress, as if defending access to it. Its surface was moving sluggishly, like a kind of coagulating ooze, but the first craft, which it had swallowed up a moment before, was nowhere to be seen.

"Base to RC 8, do you hear RC 4, over."

"RC 8 to base, negative. Shifting to interferential frequency. Attention RC 4, this is RC 8, come in RC 4. RC 4!" They could hear only the pilot's voice. "RC 4 not responding, shifting to infrared frequency. Attention RC 4, this is RC 8, come in. RC 4 not responding, I'll try to probe the cloud by radar . . ."

Not so much as the sound of breathing could be heard on the dimly lit bridge. Everyone was on tenterhooks. The image, left to its own devices, did not change; the rocky crest jutted from the sea of black like an island in the middle of an ocean of ink. High in the sky were some last lingering fluffy white clouds filled with golden light; the disk of the sun was already touching the horizon, and in a few minutes darkness would fall.

"RC 8 to base." The pilot's voice seemed to have changed in the few seconds since he last spoke. "The radar is bouncing off pure metal, over."

"Base to RC 8, send radar image over visual channel, over."

The monitor darkened and went blank; for a moment it glowed white, then turned green, trembling with a billion flecks of light.

"The cloud is made of iron," someone said, or rather sighed, behind Rohan.

"Jason!" called the commander. "Is Jason here?"

"Yes, sir." The particle physicist came forward.

"Can I heat it up?" asked the commander calmly, pointing to the screen, and everyone understood. Jason hesitated before answering.

"RC 4 should be warned to extend his force field to the max."

"Come on, Jason. We've lost contact with him."

"Up to four thousand degrees, that shouldn't be too risky . . ."

"Thank you. Blaar, the mic! Number One to RC 8, prepare laser to fire at the cloud, low force, up to one bilierg at the epicenter, continual fire along the azimuth!"

"RC 8, continual fire to one bilierg," the pilot's voice responded immediately. For a second or so nothing happened. Then there was a flash and the central part of the cloud, occupying the lower half of the monitor, changed color. First it seemed to grow hazy, then it reddened and seethed; a kind of funnel formed with flaming sides, into which adjacent parts of the cloud fell as if being sucked in. Then the movement stopped suddenly; the cloud opened up in a huge circle, revealing chaotic accumulations of rocks, though a fine black dust like flying soot still drifted in the air.

"Number One to RC 8, descend to maximize effectiveness of fire!"

The pilot repeated the order. The cloud, forming a shifting rampart around the newly created opening, attempted to fill it, but each time its advancing arms were struck by a glowing flash, it withdrew them once again. This went on for several minutes. The situation was not sustainable. The commander didn't dare strike the cloud with the full force of the cannon, since the second plane was someplace deep inside it. Rohan guessed what Horpach was counting on: He hoped that the other pilot would escape into the area that had been cleared. But there was still no sign of him. RC 8 now hovered almost motionless, blasting the churning edges of the dark circle with the blinding beams of its lasers. The sky overhead was still quite bright, but the rocks below were gradually filling with shadow. The sun was setting. All at once, the thickening gloom down in the valley shuddered in an extraordinary burst of light. Dirty red, like the mouth of a volcano seen through the turmoil of an eruption, it covered the entire scene in a quivering shroud. Now all that could be seen were blacknesses flowing into one another, fire raging and spitting deep within. This was the substance of the cloud, whatever it might be, attacking the first craft after it had engulfed it, and burning up with a terrifying intensity against its force field.

Rohan looked over at the commander, who stood as if lifeless, his expressionless face bathed in the flickering glow from the monitor. The churning black mass, and the fire simmering

99

deep within it and only occasionally intensifying into a ragged flame, filled the center of the screen. In the distance was the rocky peak awash in the cold crimson of last light, which at the present moment was uncannily like that of Earth. This made the spectacle playing out inside the cloud all the more improbable. Rohan waited; the captain's face showed nothing. Yet he had to make a decision: either order the higher craft to go to the assistance of the other one, or, leaving the latter to its fate, tell the pilot to continue north-east.

Then something unexpected happened. Whether the pilot of the lower plane trapped inside the cloud lost his head, or whether some emergency had occurred on that craft—whatever the case, the roiling black was lit up by a flash with a blinding white center, while long skeins of cloud driven apart by the explosion dispersed in every direction. The shock wave was so powerful the entire image shook in rhythm with the jolting of RC 8 caused by the blast. Then the blackness returned, gathered, concentrating itself, and that was the only thing there was.

The commander bent down and said something to the radio operator at the microphones, but so quietly that Rohan couldn't hear; the operator, however, repeated his words immediately, almost shouting:

"Prepare the antiprotons! Full force, fire at the cloud, continual fire!"

The pilot repeated the order. All at once one of the technicians watching a secondary monitor that showed what was going on behind the craft exclaimed:

"Attention! RC 8—move upwards! Move upwards! Upwards!"

From the previously empty sky to the west a swirling black billow was approaching with the rapidity of a hurricane. For an instant it formed a lateral part of the main cloud, but it quickly broke away from it and, leaving behind a trail of instantly extended side branches, shot steeply upwards. The pilot, who had spotted this a split second before the warning, moved up in a direct vertical line, gaining altitude, but the cloud pursued him, sending black columns into the sky. The pilot turned his fire from one column to another; when the nearest black whirl took a direct hit it split in two and darkened. All of a sudden the entire image began to shake.

At that moment, when part of the cloud was beginning to encroach on the radio waves of the transmission, impairing communication between plane and base, the pilot must have used the antimatter cannon for the first time. The entire atmosphere of the planet turned into a single sea of fire as it was struck; the crimson glow of the sunset vanished just like that; through the zigzagging interference, for a moment longer the black cloud loomed hazily along with the smoking columns above, which swelled as they turned white. Then another, even more terrifying explosion sent glowing showers of fire over the jumble of rocks as they disappeared in wreaths of steam and gas. This was the last thing they saw; the following second the entire picture shuddered, glittered with sparks of static, and vanished. On the darkened bridge there was only a blank white screen illuminating the deathly pale faces of the watchers.

Horpach ordered the radio operators to call both craft, while he, Rohan, Jason, and the others moved into the adjacent navigation cabin.

"What do you think this cloud is?" he asked without any preamble.

"It's composed of metallic particles. Some sort of suspension, remotely controlled, with a homogeneous center," said Jason.

"Gaarb?"

"I agree."

"Does anyone have any suggestions? No? So much the better. Chief Engineer, which supercopter is in better shape, ours or the one we took from the *Condor*?"

"Both are in working order, sir. But personally I'd go with ours."

"Very well. Mr. Rohan, if I'm not mistaken you had a yen to go outside the force field. Now's your chance. You'll have a complement of eighteen men, a double issue of automatons, mobile lasers and antiprotons ... Do we have anything else?" No one responded. "Right, for now no one's invented anything more powerful than an antimatter cannon ... You'll set off at 4.31 hours, which is to say at sunrise, and you'll try and locate the crater to the northeast that Regnar mentioned in his last report. You'll land there in an open force field. On the way, fire at anything from maximum distance. No waiting, observing, no experimentation. And no holding back on firepower. If you lose contact with me, continue your mission. When you find the crater, land there, but carefully, so you don't come down on any human beings ... I imagine they must be someplace here—" he pointed to a location on a map covering the entire wall—"in this region marked in red. It's just a sketch, but we have nothing better."

"What am I to do after we land, commander? Should I look for them?"

"I leave that to your discretion. Just remember one thing: You mustn't fire at anything within a 30-mile radius of this spot, because our people could be down below."

"No land-based targets?"

"No targets at all. Up to this boundary," said the captain, with a movement of the hand dividing the area shown on the map into two parts, "you can use your weapons offensively. Beyond this line, you can only defend yourselves with your force field. Mr. Jason! How much can the supercopter's force field withstand?"

"As much as a million atmospheres per square centimeter, sir."

"'As much as'? What does that mean? Are you trying to sell me the thing? I'm asking how much. Five million? Twenty?"

Horpach's tone was utterly calm; this disposition of his was what people on board most dreaded. Jason cleared his throat.

"The field has been tested to two and a half ..."

"Well that's something else. Do you hear, Mr. Rohan? If the cloud attacks up to this boundary, get out of the way. Best of all upwards. Though the fact is, I can't predict everything ..." He looked at his watch.

"Eight hours after your departure I'm going to call you on all frequencies. If that's not successful, we'll try to make contact either via Trojan satellites, or optically. We'll laser in Morse. I've never known that not to work. But let's try and anticipate beyond what we've known. If the lasers also fail, three hours after that you'll take off and return. If I'm not here—"

"You're planning to fly elsewhere, sir?"

"Don't interrupt, Mr. Rohan. No, I'm not planning to fly anywhere else, but not everything depends on us. If I'm not here, enter into planetary orbit. Have you already done that in a supercopter?"

"Yes, sir, twice, on Delta Lyrae."

"Very good. Then you know it's a little complicated, but entirely feasible. It has to be a stationary orbit; Stroem will give you the exact data before takeoff. You'll wait for me in this orbit for 36 hours. If you receive no sign from me in that time, return to the planet. Fly to the *Condor* and try to get it operational. I know how things look there. Still, you won't have any other options. If you manage that trick, return to base in the *Condor* and report on what has happened here. Any questions?"

"Yes. May I attempt to make contact with the beings, the being, directing the cloud, if I should succeed in locating it, or them?"

"I leave that up to you as well. Either way, the risk has to remain within reasonable bounds. I know nothing, of course, but I have the feeling that the command center is not situated on the surface of the planet. Besides, I find its very existence problematic."

"What do you mean?"

"Well, we have permanent radio monitoring covering the entire electromagnetic spectrum. If anyone were steering the cloud with the aid of radio waves we'd have picked up the signals."

"Perhaps the center is within the cloud itself."

"Maybe. I can't say. Mr. Jason, is it possible there exist methods of remote communication other than electromagnetic?"

"You're asking for my opinion, sir? No. There are no such methods."

"Your opinion? What else could I be asking for?"

"What I know isn't the same as what exists. What could exist. We don't know of any such methods. That's all."

"Telepathy," someone standing behind put in.

"I have nothing to say on that subject," Jason replied drily. "In any case, in the known universe nothing of that kind has been discovered."

"Gentlemen, we have no time for fruitless discussion. Take your men, Mr. Rohan, and get the supercopter ready. Stroem will give you the ecliptic details of the orbit in an hour's time. Mr. Stroem, please calculate a fixed orbit with an apogee of three thousand."

"Yes, captain."

The commander opened the door to the bridge.

"Mr. Terner, how are things going? You don't have anything?"

"Nothing, sir. I mean, crackling. A lot of static, nothing else."

"No trace of the transmission spectrum?"

"None."

That means neither of the two planes is using their weapons now—that they've stopped fighting, thought Rohan. If they'd been firing their lasers, or even just their induction cannon, the *Invincible*'s sensors would have detected it from hundreds of miles away.

Rohan was too absorbed in the drama of the situation to be nervous about the mission he'd been given by the commander. In fact, he wouldn't even have had time to worry about it. That night he didn't sleep a wink. All the copter's systems needed to be checked, then it had to be loaded with additional tons of fuel, supplies, and weaponry; they barely made it before the assigned takeoff time. The double-decker, seven thousand tonne craft rose into the air, throwing up clouds of dust, and moved off due north-east just as the tip of the sun's red disk appeared over the horizon. Right from takeoff Rohan ascended to nine miles; once in the stratosphere he would be able to accelerate to maximum speed, besides which there was less chance of an encounter with the black cloud. At least that was what he calculated. Perhaps he was right, perhaps it was just a matter of good fortune; in any case, less than an hour later they landed in the sand-filled crater in the slanting rays of the sun. Shadows still filled its lower reaches.

Before the columns of hot gas blasting downwards had begun to stir up billows of sand, the men watching the TV monitors warned the navigation cabin that in the northern part of the crater they had spotted something suspicious. The bulky craft stopped in place, trembling slightly as if it were on an invisible spring, and the spot in question was observed closely from an altitude of fifteen hundred feet.

The magnified image on the monitor showed an ashy red background against which tiny rectangles were arranged with geometric precision around a large one that was steel gray. At the same moment as Gaarb and Ballmin, who were with him at the controls, Rohan recognized the vehicles of Regnar's expedition.

Wasting no time, they landed a short distance away, maintaining all cautionary measures. The copter's telescopic legs were still bending and settling down evenly when they threw open the bottom hatch and sent out two recon vehicles under the protection of a mobile force field. The inside of the crater resembled a shallow bowl with a jagged rim. The central cone of the volcano was caked in a ruddy black crust of lava.

It took the vehicles a few minutes to cross the mile or so they had to travel. Radio contact was crystal clear. Rohan talked with Gaarb, who was in the lead transporter.

"We're coming to the edge of the rise, we'll see them in just a minute," Gaarb repeated several times. A moment later he shouted: "They're there! I can see them!"

Then more calmly:

"It looks like everything's in order. One, two, three, four—all the vehicles are in place. Though why are they parked in the sun?"

"But what about the men? Can you see them?" Rohan kept asking, standing at the microphone, his eyes narrowed.

"Yes. Something's moving there ... It's two people ... a third ... and someone lying in the shade ... I can see them, Rohan!"

His voice grew fainter; Rohan heard him say something to his driver. A dull boom indicated that a smoke flare had been sent up. Gaarb's voice returned:

"We're sending them a hello ... The smoke's blown in their direction a bit ... It'll clear in a moment ... Jarg—what's going on there? What! What do you mean? Hey! You over there!"

His shouts filled the entire cabin then suddenly broke off. Rohan heard the sound of engines cutting out; there were running steps, muffled exclamations in the distance, a shout, another, then silence.

"Hello! Gaarb! Gaarb!" he repeated, his lips trembling. The footsteps on the sand approached, and there was a creaking sound.

"Rohan," came Gaarb's voice, out of breath and altered. "Rohan! It's the same as with Kertelen! They're unconscious, they don't recognize us, they're not saying anything ... Rohan, do you hear?!"

"Yes ... Are they all like that?"

"It looks that way ... I don't know yet, Jarg and Terner are checking them one by one."

"Wait, what about the force field?"

"It's been turned off. It's not there. I don't know. They must have turned it off."

"Are there any signs of a fight?"

"No, nothing. Their vehicles are all here, untouched—and they're all just sitting or lying there, you can shake them— what? What is it?"

Rohan heard faint sounds interrupted by a protracted whimpering. He tightened his jaw, but he was unable to overcome a sickening sensation that churned his stomach.

"Great heavens, it's Gralev!" Gaarb exclaimed. "Gralev, man! Don't you know me?!"

His breathing intensified, filling the cabin.

"Him too ... ," he gasped. He was silent for a moment, as if he was gathering his strength.

"Rohan ... I don't know if we'll be able to manage on our own. They'll all need to be taken from here. Send more men."

"Right away."

An hour later, a ghastly procession came to a halt beneath the metal hull of the supercopter. Of the twenty-two men of the expedition, only eighteen remained; the fate of the other four was unknown. The majority allowed themselves to be led voluntarily, without putting up any resistance, but five of them had to be brought in by force as they'd been unwilling to leave the place where they had been found. Five stretchers made their way to an improvised sick bay on the copter's lower deck. The remaining thirteen men, whose masklike faces appalled the others, were led into a separate cabin, where they let themselves be laid on bunks without protest. Someone else had to undress them and remove their boots, since they were as helpless as babies. Rohan, a silent witness of this scene as he stood between the double rows of berths, saw that while most of the rescued men remained passive and calm, a few of them—those who had had to be brought forcibly—were wailing in eerie voices.

He left all of them in the care of the physician, while he himself sent all the resources at his disposal in search of the missing men. In fact he was well equipped at this point, since he made use of the abandoned vehicles, manning them from his own team. He had just dispatched the final patrol when the radio operator called him into the cabin: They had made contact with the *Invincible*.

He wasn't even surprised that this was possible. It was as if nothing could surprise him anymore. He gave Horpach a succinct account of what had happened.

"Who's missing?" the commander asked.

"Regnar himself, Bennigsen, Korotka, and Mead. What's the situation with the planes?" Rohan inquired in turn.

"I have no information."

"And the cloud?"

"I sent the third RC out this morning. It came back an hour ago. There was no sign of the cloud."

"Nothing? Nothing at all?"

"Nothing."

"Nor the planes?"

"Nothing."

LAUDA'S HYPOTHESIS

Dr. Lauda knocked on the door of the captain's cabin. When he entered, he saw Horpach plotting something on a photogrammetric map.

"What is it?" the latter asked without looking up.

"I wanted to tell you something, captain."

"Is it urgent? We're taking off in fifteen minutes."

"I'm not sure. I think I'm starting to understand what's happening here," said Lauda.

The commander set aside his compasses. Their eyes met. The biologist was no younger than the captain. It was unusual that he'd still been allowed to fly. He must have really wanted to. He looked more like a seasoned mechanic than a scientist.

"You think so, doctor? I'm listening."

"There's life in the ocean," said the biologist. "In the ocean there is, but on land there isn't."

"What do you mean? There was life on land too; Ballmin found traces."

"Right. But they were over five million years old. After that all life on land was wiped out. What I'm going to say will sound far-fetched, captain, and I don't really have any proof, but . . . so it goes. Imagine that at a certain time, millions of years ago in fact, a rocket from another system landed here. Perhaps from the region of a nova."

He was speaking faster now, but evenly.

"We know that before the explosion of Zeta Lyrae, the sixth planet of its system was inhabited by intelligent life. They had a technologically highly developed civilization. Let's suppose that a Lyran scout ship landed here, and there was a crash. Or some other accident in which the entire crew perished. An explosion in the reactor, say, a chain reaction … in any case, what was left of the craft that landed on Regis no longer had any living being on board. All that survived were the automatons. These were not like ours. They weren't humanoid. The Lyrans probably were not humanoid either. So the automatons came through intact and left the ship. They were highly specialized homeostatic mechanisms capable of enduring in the harshest of conditions. There was no longer anyone in charge of them, giving them orders. Those of them that most closely resembled the Lyrans from the point of view of intelligence may have attempted to repair the ship, though in the given situation such a thing was pointless. But you know how it is. A repair robot will repair what's it's supposed to repair, regardless of whether it's useful to anyone or not. Later, though, other automatons came to dominate. They became independent of the first ones. It may have been that the local fauna tried to attack them. There were lizardlike reptilians here, so there must also have been predators, and certain kinds of predator will attack anything that moves. The automatons began to fight with them, and defeated them. For this struggle they had to adapt. They altered themselves to be as well suited as possible to conditions on the planet. A crucial factor, in my view, is that the automatons possessed the ability to manufacture other automatons, according to their needs. So for, let's say, battling flying saurians they needed flying mechanisms. Of course, I have no concrete details. I'm speaking as if I were imagining a similar situation in conditions of natural evolution. There may not have been any flying saurians; maybe they were burrowing creatures that lived underground. I can't say. In any case, with the passage of time the mechanisms that existed on land became perfectly adapted to the conditions there—and they succeeded in overcoming all forms of animal life on the planet. Plant life too."

"Plant life? Why is that?"

"I'm not sure. I could propose various hypotheses, but I'd rather not. Besides, I haven't gotten to the most important part. During their time on the planet these descendant mechanisms, after however many hundreds of generations, ceased to resemble those that had given them their beginning—which is to say, they were no longer like products of Lyran civilization. You understand? This means that inanimate evolution had begun. The evolution of mechanical devices. What is the foremost principle of homeostasis? To survive in changing circumstances, however difficult and hostile these may be. The major threat to the later forms of this evolution of self-organizing metal systems was not that presented by local animals or plants. They needed to find sources of energy and materials from which they could produce replacement parts and new organisms. And so they developed something like mining, in search of metal ores. Initially the descendants of those that came here on the hypothetical ship were undoubtedly powered by nuclear energy. But on Regis there are no radioactive elements whatsoever. This power source, then, was closed to them. They had to look for another. There must have been a severe energy crisis, and I believe it led to conflict among the devices. A struggle for survival, for existence, quite simply. After all, that's what evolution is about. Selection. The mechanisms that were highly developed in terms of intelligence, but ill suited for survival, because of their dimensions let's say, which required large quantities of energy, were unable to compete with others that were less advanced as far as intelligence is concerned, yet were more economical and efficient when it came to energy ..."

"Just a minute, doctor. Never mind how far-fetched this may be, in evolution, the game of evolution, the being with the more highly developed nervous system always wins, isn't that so? In this case, rather than a nervous system it's an electrical one, shall we say, but the principle remains the same."

"That's true, captain, but only in relation to homogeneous organisms that have arisen on a planet in a natural way, not those coming from other systems."

"I don't follow."

"It's simply that the biochemical conditions for the functioning of beings on Earth were and are always virtually the same. Algae, amoebas, plants, lower and higher animals—all are constructed of almost identical cells, all have virtually the same metabolism—based on protein—and in the face of such an even start, the distinguishing factor is what you said. It's not the only one, but it's at the very least one of the most important. Here, though, things were different. The most highly developed mechanisms that landed on Regis got their energy from their own radioactive reserves, whereas simpler devices, certain small repair systems for example, may have possessed solar batteries. If so, they would have been in a highly privileged position relative to the others."

"But the higher mechanisms could have simply helped themselves to their solar batteries. Besides, where is this debate leading? Maybe it's not even worth talking about, Dr. Lauda."

"No, this is the crux of the matter, it's vital, since in my opinion what came about here was inanimate evolution of a very particular nature, begun in exceptional circumstances that were brought about by happenstance. In a word, I see it so: In this evolution the victors were firstly systems that miniaturized themselves most effectively, and secondly those that were sedentary. The first gave rise to the so-called black clouds. Personally I believe these are tiny pseudo-insects that in case of need, for mutual self-interest as it were, are capable of joining into large superordinate systems. Precisely in the form of clouds. This was the direction in which the mobile mechanisms developed. The sedentary ones in turn gave rise to the bizarre species of metallic vegetation found in the ruins of what we've been calling cities . . ."

"So according to you these are not cities?"

"Of course not. They're not cities at all, they're merely large agglomerations of sedentary mechanisms, inanimate formations able to multiply, and absorbing solar energy by means of their own kind of organs . . . I suspect that's what the little triangular plates must be."

"So you believe the 'city' is still flourishing?"

"No. I have the impression that for some reason unknown to us this city, or rather metal forest, lost its struggle for existence and now is no more than rusting remains. Only one form has survived: the mobile beings that have taken over all the land on the planet."

"Why?"

"I don't know. I considered various possible calculations. It may be that in the course of the last three million years the sun of Regis III cooled faster than before, such that the large sedentary 'organisms' were no longer able to acquire sufficient amounts of energy. But those are only vague suppositions."

"Let's say you're right. Do you think these clouds have some control center on the surface of the planet, or underground?"

"I don't believe anything like that exists. It may be that the micromechanisms themselves constitute such a center, a kind of inanimate brain, when they join together in a particular way. Separating may be advantageous to them. They comprise loosely organized swarms, thanks to which they can remain permanently in sunlight or chase after storm clouds, because it's entirely possible they draw their energy from atmospheric discharges. But when danger strikes, or more generally some sudden change threatens their existence, they come together ... "

"But something has to prompt this reaction of linking with one another. Also, at these times of swarming where is the extraordinarily complex memory of the entire system located? After all, an electrical brain is smarter than the sum of its parts, Dr. Lauda. How is it possible that these parts could fall back into place after the thing has been dismantled? First off, a plan of the entire brain would have to come into existence."

"Not necessarily. It would be enough if every part contained a memory of the other parts it was directly attached to. Let's say part number one has to join together with six others, that particular areas of their surfaces come into contact. Each of these 'knows' the same about itself. In this manner the amount of information contained in an individual part may be negligible, but other than that all that's needed is a particular trigger, a signal that says something like, 'attention! danger!,' at which they all enter into the necessary configurations and the 'brain' is instantly constituted. This is only a primitive schematic, though, captain. I suspect that the matter is more complicated, if only because the parts for sure often end up being destroyed, yet this cannot affect the actions of the whole ..."

"Very well. We don't have time to pore over any more details. Do you see any concrete conclusions your hypothesis suggests for us?"

"In a certain sense yes, though negative ones. Millions of years of mechanical evolution, and a phenomenon that humans have never before encountered in the Galaxy. Please consider the most fundamental matter. All the machines we are familiar with serve someone else, not themselves. Thus, from a human perspective the existence of the vast metallic jungles of Regis, or its iron clouds, are quite pointless—in the same sense, it's true, that cactuses in the deserts of Earth could be called pointless. The essential thing is that they are perfectly adapted for combat with living beings. I have the impression that they killed only at the very beginnings of the struggle, when the land here teemed with life. The energy expended on killing proved to be uneconomical. For that reason they use other methods, the results of which include the catastrophe of the *Condor*, Kertelen's accident, and now the devastation wrought on Regnar's team."

"What methods?"

"I'm not exactly sure how it works. I can only express my personal judgment: Kertelen's case involves the obliteration of almost the entire contents of a human brain. The same would no doubt be true of an animal's brain too. Living creatures crippled in such a way would naturally perish. It's a method that is simpler, quicker, and more efficient than killing. The conclusion I draw from this is unfortunately a pessimistic one. Maybe even that is not putting it strongly enough ... Our situation is incomparably worse than theirs, for several reasons at once. First, a living being can be destroyed much more easily than a mechanism or a technical device. Furthermore, they evolved in conditions in which they were simultaneously fighting with living creatures and with their metal brothers, intelligent automatons. In other words, they were waging war on two fronts at the same time, battling all the adaptive mechanisms of living systems and all manifestations of intelligence in thinking machines. The result of these struggles, which went on for millions of years, has to be an exceptional universalism and a perfection in the operations of the one destroying. I'm afraid that in order to defeat them we would have to annihilate virtually every last one of them, and that is almost impossible."

"You think so?"

"I do. I mean, it goes without saying that with the right concentration of means you could blow up the whole planet ... But that is not our task, not to mention the fact that we lack the power. The situation is basically unique, since, as I see it, we are actually superior in terms of intelligence. These mechanisms are nowhere close to being any kind of mental powerhouse, they're simply perfectly suited to the conditions of the planet—to destroying anything that is intelligent and anything that is alive. They themselves are inanimate. For this reason, that which for them is harmless, for us may be lethal."

"How can you be so sure they don't possess reason?"

"I could be evasive here, hide behind my lack of knowledge, but let me tell you that if there's anything at all I'm certain of, it's that. Why do I say they lack a powerful intellect? Goodness! If they were intelligent, they'd already have polished us off. Go over in your mind all the successive events that took place on Regis since the moment we landed, and you'll see that they're operating without any strategic plan. They attack from one opportunity to the next."

"Hmm ... What about the way they prevented Regnar from being in contact with us, then the attack on the recon planes ..."

"They're simply doing what they've done for millennia. I mean, the higher automatons that they wiped out must have communicated with one another precisely by means of radio waves. Obstructing these kinds of exchange of information, disrupting communication, was one of their first tasks. The solution was more or less self-evident, since a metal cloud makes a better blocker than anything else in the world. But now? What are we to do next? We need to protect ourselves and our automatons, our machines, without which we would be nothing. Whereas they have full freedom of maneuver, they possess virtually inexhaustible resources for regenerating themselves, they can multiply if we destroy a part of them, and on top of everything they're invulnerable to everything that is fatal to life. Our most violent means have become necessary—an antimatter strike ... But it's not possible to attack all of them in such a way. Have you noticed how they behave when they're hit? They simply scatter ... Besides which, we have to remain permanently protected by a force field, thus limiting our strategic options, while they can disperse at will and move from one location to another ... And if we were to annihilate them on this continent, they'd simply move to another. Though when it comes down to it, it's not our job to annihilate them all. I think we should leave the planet."

"I see."

"Yes. Because if our adversaries are the products of inanimate and probably unthinking evolution, we cannot regard the problem in terms of revenge or payback for the *Condor*, for the fate of its crew. That would be no different than whipping the ocean for having sunk a ship and drowned its sailors."

"There'd be a lot of sense in what you're suggesting if things really were that way," said Horpach, rising to his feet. He rested both hands on the map. "But this is after all a hypothesis, and we can't return with nothing more than hypotheses. What we need is certainty. Not revenge, but certainty. An accurate diagnosis, the establishment of facts. If we manage it, if I can secure on board the *Invincible* some samples of this, this flying mechanical fauna, assuming they actually exist—at such a time I'll of course accept that we have nothing more to do here. At that point it will be up to the base to determine how to proceed. Incidentally, there's no guarantee these formations will remain on the planet; maybe they'll develop and begin to threaten space travel in general in this part of the Galaxy."

"Even if that were to happen, it would take hundreds of thousands of years, more likely millions. Commander, I'm afraid you're still reasoning as if we were faced with a thinking opponent. Something that was once the tool of rational beings became independent after they disappeared, and with the passage of millions of years effectively grew to be part of the natural forces of the planet. Life remained in the ocean, because mechanical evolution does not extend there, but it doesn't allow those life forms access to the land. This explains the moderate amount of oxygen in the atmosphere—it's produced by oceanic algae—and also why the continents look the way they do. They're deserts, because these organisms do not build anything, possess no civilization, in general have nothing whatsoever except themselves, create nothing of value. This is why we should treat them like a force of nature. Nature likewise does not appraise, it offers no values. These beings are simply themselves, they endure, and they act in such a way as to be able to endure further ..."

"How do you explain the destruction of the planes? They were protected by force fields."

"A force field can be overcome by another force field. Besides, captain, in order to be able to wipe out the entire memory contained in a person's brain in a split second, you'd need to instantaneously assemble around his head a magnetic field of a power that even we would have trouble generating, with all the means we have on board. You'd need some kind of gigantic converters, transformers, electromagnets ..." **121**

"And you think they have all that?"

"Far from it! They have nothing. They're simply little building blocks that the exigencies of a moment use to construct what's needed. A signal comes in saying, 'threat!' Something has appeared that can be detected by the changes it induces, for example alterations in the electrostatic field. At once the flying swarm forms into this 'cloud-brain' or whatever it is, and its collective memory is constituted: Beings like this have appeared before, we dealt with them in such and such a way, after which they were exterminated ... And they repeat the same course of action."

"Very well," said Horpach, who for some time now had stopped hearing what the elderly biologist was saying. "I'll delay the takeoff. We'll call a council. I'd rather not, because there's likely to be a huge discussion, scientific passions will flare, but I don't see any other option. In half an hour, in the main library, Dr. Lauda."

"Let them convince me I'm wrong, and you'll have one truly contented man on board," the doctor said evenly, and left the cabin as soundlessly as he had entered. Horpach straightened, went up to the intercom on the wall and, pressing the key for the internal speaker system, summoned all the scientists in turn.

As it turned out, the majority of the specialists harbored thoughts along the same lines as Lauda's; he was merely the first to have formulated them so categorically. The only argument that flared up concerned the question of whether the cloud had a mind or not. The cyberneticians tended to see it as a thinking system with the capacity for strategic action. Lauda came under sharp attack; Horpach understood that the virulence of the onslaught was brought about not so much by Lauda's hypothesis itself as by the fact that he had discussed it first with the commander instead of with his colleagues. Despite all the ties connecting them to the crew, the scientists on board still constituted something of a "state within a state," and they observed a certain unspoken code of behavior.

Kronotos, the Chief Cybernetician, asked how in Lauda's opinion the "cloud" had learned to attack humans if it was devoid of intelligence.

"That's easy," the biologist came back. "It did nothing else for millions of years. I'm referring to its war with the original inhabitants of Regis. They were creatures with a central nervous system. They learned to attack them the same way a terrestrial insect attacks its victim. They do so with a precision comparable to that of a wasp injecting toxin into the ganglia of a grasshopper or a beetle. It's not intelligence, it's instinct."

"But how did they know to attack the planes? They'd never encountered such things before."

"That we cannot know, doctor. Like I said, they fought on two fronts, against the living inhabitants of Regis and the non-living ones, meaning other automatons. By the very nature of things the latter must have used various kinds of energy for the purposes of defense and attack."

"But if they didn't include flying devices . . ."

"I think I see what Dr. Kronotos is getting at," put in Saurahan, the Deputy Chief Cybernetician.

"The large robots, the macroautomatons, communicated with one another in order to coordinate; the easiest way to destroy them was through isolation, separation, and the most effective means of doing that was by preventing communication."

123

"The question is not whether particular aspects of the cloud's behavior can be explained without recourse to a hypothesis of intelligence," rejoined Kronotos. "We're not bound by Occam's razor. It's not our job, at least right now, to come up with a hypothesis that explains everything in the most sparing manner, but rather one that will enable us to act in the safest way possible. For this reason it's better to assume the cloud may possess intelligence—that would be more prudent. It'll lead us to act more cautiously. Whereas if we follow Dr. Lauda in accepting that the cloud does not have intelligence, while in reality it does, we could end up paying a terrible price for our mistake. I say this not as a theoretician, but above all as a strategist."

"I'm not sure who you're trying to defeat, the cloud or me," Lauda responded levelly. "I'm not arguing for a lack of caution, but the cloud has no intelligence except of the kind possessed by an insect, and actually not even that of an individual insect so much as, let's say, an ant colony. I mean, if this were not so we would already be dead."

"Prove it."

"We're not the cloud's first opponent of the species *homo sapiens*: Remember, the *Condor* was here before us. In order to penetrate inside the force field, all these microscopic 'flies' would need to do is bury into the sand. The field only reaches to its surface. They had encountered the force fields of the *Condor*, so they could have learned such a form of attack. Whereas in fact they did nothing of the sort. So either the cloud is stupid, or it's acting instinctively."

Kronotos refused to back down, but at this point Horpach intervened, suggesting that they postpone further discussion. He asked for concrete proposals arising from what had been determined with a high degree of probability. Nygren asked if it would be possible to shield people by giving them metal helmets that would prevent the operation of a magnetic field. The physicists, however, concluded that this would not be effective, since a very powerful field would create eddy currents that would heat the helmet to high temperatures. When it began to burn, the wearer would have to take it off, with obvious consequences.

By now it was nighttime. In one corner of the room Horpach was talking with Lauda and the physicians; the cyberneticians were conversing separately.

"I still find it curious that the beings with greater intelligence, these macroautomatons, didn't come out on top," one of them was saying. "This would be the exception that proves the rule stating that evolution moves in the direction of more complexity, of perfecting homeostasis ... of information and the exploitation of information."

"These automatons didn't stand a chance, precisely because they were so highly developed and complex from the get-go," replied Saurahan. "Think about it: They were highly specialized for the purposes of collaboration with their constructors, the Lyrans, and once the Lyrans went away they were crippled, as it were—deprived of leadership. Whereas the forms that gave rise to today's 'flies' (I'm not remotely suggesting they already existed back then, in fact I don't think that's even possible, they must have come into being much later), those forms were relatively primitive and for that reason had many possible avenues for development ahead of them."

"There may have been an even more significant factor," added Dr. Sax, who had joined them. "We're talking about mechanisms, and mechanisms never demonstrate the same self-repairing tendencies as living creatures, living tissue, which remakes itself after it's wounded. A macroautomaton, even if it were capable of repairing another of its kind, would require tools for the job, a whole shop in fact. So in order to cripple them, all you'd need to do would be to cut them off from their tools. At that point they'd be easy prey for the flying forms that were much less vulnerable."

"That's extremely interesting," Saurahan said out of the blue. "It would suggest that automatons need to be constructed entirely differently than the way we do it, for them to be truly universal. We should begin with tiny elementary building blocks, pseudocells, which are mutually replaceable."

"That's not such a new idea," smiled Sax. "The evolution of living forms develops in just such a way, and not by chance either. For the same reason, the fact that the cloud is composed of these interchangeable parts is also not by accident. It's a question of material: A damaged macroautomaton requires replacement parts that can only be produced by a highly developed form of industry, whereas a system made up of a handful of little crystals or thermistors, or some other kind of simple links—such a system could be destroyed without any ill effect, because it would be immediately replaced by a billion others like it."

Seeing he could not expect much from them, Horpach left the gathering; the others were so engrossed in their conversations they barely noticed. He headed for the bridge to inform Rohan's team about the hypothesis of "inanimate evolution." It was dark by the time the *Invincible* made contact with the supercopter in the crater. Gaarb was at the microphone.

"We have only seven men," he said, "including two physicians who are tending to the casualties. The others are sleeping right now, except for the radio operator, who's here with me. Yes, we have full force field cover. But Rohan isn't back yet."

"Isn't back yet?! When did he leave?"

"Around six in the afternoon. He took six vehicles and all the rest of the team. We agreed he'd return after sunset. The sun went down ten minutes ago."

"Are you in radio contact with him?"

"It cut out about an hour ago."

"Why didn't you inform me of this at once, Mr. Gaarb?"

"Because Rohan was certain communication would be interrupted since they were entering one of the deep ravines, you know, sir. The sides are all overgrown with that metal crap that creates reflections so bad there's really no chance of receiving a signal."

"Let me know at once when Rohan comes back ... He'll answer for this. That way we could end up losing everyone ..."

The captain was saying something else when Gaarb interrupted him with an exclamation:

"They're coming, commander! I see their lights, they're moving up the slope, it's Rohan ... one, two—or no, just one vehicle ... I'll find out right away what the situation is."

"I'll be waiting."

Seeing the light from the headlamps rocking back and forth close to the ground, their beams repeatedly hitting the camp then disappearing in the folds of the terrain, Gaarb grabbed hold of a flare gun and fired twice into the sky. The effect was immediate—all those who'd been sleeping leaped to their feet. In the meantime the approaching vehicle described an arc, the radio operator on duty made an opening in the force field, and the dust-covered transporter rumbled across the strip of ground indicated by the blue lights and came to a halt at the foot of the dune on which the supercopter was perched. Gaarb was horrified to see that the new arrival was the radio vehicle, a small three-man reconnaissance amphibian. In the light of hurriedly mounted floodlights, along with the others he had run toward the vehicle as it drove in. Before it had properly come to a stop, a man jumped out. He was wearing a torn jump suit; his face was so dirty with mud and blood that Gaarb didn't recognize him till he spoke.

"Gaarb," he groaned, grabbing the scientist by the arm. His legs folded under him. Others rushed forward to hold him up, shouting:

"What happened? Where are the others?"

"The others ... are ... gone ... All of them ... ," whispered Rohan, and passed out as they held him.

Around midnight the physicians managed to bring him back to consciousness. Lying beneath the aluminum roof of the barracks in an oxygen tent, he recounted the story that half an hour later Gaarb telegraphed to the *Invincible*.

ROHAN'S TEAM

The convoy that Rohan had led consisted of two large ener-gobots, four all-terrain caterpillar transporters and a small amphibian craft. Rohan traveled in this last vehicle, along with the driver Jarg and Terner the bosun. They moved along in the configuration called for by degree three procedures. First came the energobot with no passengers, behind it Rohan's recon amphibian, after that four vehicles carrying two men each, then in the rear the second energobot, which along with the one in the lead provided a force field for the entire group.

Rohan had decided on the expedition because while he was still in the crater, with the aid of "electric bloodhounds"—olfactometric sensors—he had hit on the trails of the four men missing from Regnar's team. It was plain that if they weren't found, they would die of hunger or thirst as they wandered about the rocky, pathless landscape, more helpless than children. They rode the first few miles guided by the sensors. At the entrance to one of the broad, shallow ravines they had been passing in this region, around seven they spotted clear footprints left in the mud of a drying creek. They made out three sets of prints perfectly preserved in the soft wet earth, which had dried only slightly during the day; there was also a fourth set, less distinct because it had been partially washed away by the water that trickled among the boulders. These traces, with their characteristic shape, had obviously been made by the heavy boots of the men from Regnar's team as they entered the ravine. A little further on they faded away on the rock, but of course this did not deter Rohan, because he could see that the sides of the ravine grew steeper and steeper as they went. For this reason it was unlikely that the fugitives, suffering from amnesia as they were, would have managed to climb up out of the place. Rohan was counting on finding them soon further down the ravine, where it was impossible to see ahead beyond the numerous twists and turns. After a brief consultation the column moved on till it reached a place where both sides of the ravine were overgrown with the strange metal bushes, unusually close-packed at this point. They were squat, brush-like formations between three and five feet high. They grew out of cracks in the bare rock that were filled with a blackish soil. To begin with, only isolated bushes appeared; further on, they merged into an unbroken jungle that formed a rusty, bristling layer blanketing both slopes of the ravine almost to the bottom, where a thin filament of water ran between large boulders.

Here and there among the bushes, the entrances to caves could be seen. From some of them narrow rivulets of water flowed; others were dry, or seemed to have dried up. Rohan's team tried to look into those that were located relatively low down, shining their flashlights into the interior. In one of the caves they found a large number of tiny triangular crystals partly immersed in the water dripping from the ceiling. Rohan pocketed a large handful. They had gotten about a third of a mile into the ravine, its sides growing ever steeper. Up till now the vehicles' caterpillar tracks had managed perfectly well on the sloping terrain, and since in two other places they had found more footprints in the dried mud along the stream, they were sure they were headed in the right direction. At one point, as they rounded yet another bend the radio contact they had so far managed to maintain with the supercopter deteriorated significantly, something that Rohan ascribed to the screening effect of the metal bushes. On either side of the ravine, which was seventy feet wide at the top and perhaps forty at the bottom, in places there rose almost vertical walls that were covered in a wiry mass of undergrowth like stiff black fur. There were so many bushes on each side that they formed a solid tangle reaching right up to the tops of the cliffs.

The convoy passed through two rather broad gateways in the rock; this operation took some time, as the technicians controlling the force field had to narrow its range very precisely so as not to brush against the rocks. These were severely cracked and crumbling from erosion, and if the force field had brushed against one of the pillars it could have brought about a major rockfall. They weren't worried about themselves, of course, but about the missing men, who could be injured or killed by falling rocks if they should be close by.

About an hour after radio contact was lost, closely spaced flashes began to appear on the magnetic screens of the sensors. When they tried to check the source, their compasses seemed to be malfunctioning, since they showed that the impulses were coming from every direction at once. Resorting to magnetometers and polarizers, they established that the source of fluctuations in the magnetic field were the bushes lining the walls of the ravine. It was only then that they noticed the bushes here had a different appearance than earlier: They lacked the rusty coating, they were taller and as it were blacker, as the wires or branches they were composed of were covered with bizarre swellings. Rohan decided against investigating them since he did not wish to risk opening the force field.

They quickened their speed, the impulsometers and magnetic sensors indicating activity of an increasingly varied kind. When they looked upward, they could see the air trembling in places over the entire surface of the blackish thatch, as if it were being heated to a high temperature; beyond the second gateway in the rock they noticed faint wisps drifting over the bushes like skeins of smoke. These were so far up the slope, however, that even with binoculars it was impossible to make out what they were—though Jarg, who was driving the vehicle Rohan was riding in, and who had exceptionally good eyesight, said that the smoke clouds looked like swarms of small insects.

Rohan was growing a little uneasy, since the journey was taking longer than he had anticipated, and the end of the twisting ravine was still nowhere in sight. On the other hand they were able to move faster, because they'd left behind the piles of boulders that had littered the stream bed. The stream itself had almost ceased to exist, hidden deep beneath loose rock; it was only when the vehicles came to a stop that the murmur of unseen water could be heard in the ensuing silence.

Rounding yet another bend, they came upon a gateway in the rock that was narrower than the previous ones. After taking measurements, the technicians determined that it would not be possible to pass through without turning off the force field. It was common knowledge that there were limitations to the dimensions the field could be made to assume; it always had to be some variant on a solid of revolution, in other words a sphere, ellipsoid, or hyperboloid. Before, they had managed to pass through the narrow places in the ravine by squeezing the (of course invisible) protective field into the shape of a flattened stratospheric balloon.

Now, however, there was no way of doing such a thing. Rohan consulted with Tomman the physicist and with both field technicians, and they decided jointly that they would risk turning off the force field for a brief moment, and only partially, as they passed through. First the unmanned energobot would go through with its force field off; the moment it was on the other side it would be reactivated, providing full protection in the shape of a convex shield. While the four large transporters and Rohan's small recon vehicle were driving through they would be deprived of cover only from above; the final energobot bringing up the rear would join its shield to that of the lead energobot the moment it was through, and in this way full protection would be resumed.

Everything went according to plan, and the last of the four vehicles with caterpillar tracks was just passing through the defile between the pillars of rock when the air was shaken with a bizarre judder—not a sound, but a shock, as if a rock had fallen nearby. The bristly walls of the ravine started to smoke, a black cloud rose up from there and hurtled toward the convoy at breakneck speed.

Rohan, who had decided to let the large transporters go before his amphibian, was at that moment standing and waiting for the last of them to drive through; he saw the sudden burst of black from the sides of the ravine and an immense flash up ahead, where the first energobot, now on the other side of the gateway, had turned on its force field. A section of the attacking cloud burned up on the protective shield, but its greater part passed over the flames and descended on all the machines at once. Rohan yelled to Jarg to turn on the rear energobot immediately and link its field with the front robot, since at this point

the danger of a rockslide was irrelevant. Jarg tried to do so, but
the field could not be activated. What had probably happened,
as the Chief Engineer later determined, was that the klystrons
in the machinery had overheated. If the technician had kept
them in the rising current a few seconds longer, the field would
undoubtedly have kicked in. But Jarg panicked and instead of
trying again, he jumped out of the craft. Rohan grabbed hold
of his jump suit, but Jarg pulled away, overcome by fear, and set
off running back down the ravine. When Rohan reached the
controls himself it was already too late.

The men caught in the transporters jumped down and ran
off every which way; they could barely be seen in the swirling
cloud. The scene was so unreal that Rohan no longer attempted
to do anything. (Besides, nothing could have been done—if he
had turned on the force field he would have injured them, for
they were actually trying to climb up the slopes, as if seeking
shelter in the metal jungle.) He stood passively in the abandoned vehicle and waited for the same fate to come to him.
Behind his back Terner was leaning out of the cockpit firing
compression lasers into the air, but his efforts were useless, as
the greater part of the cloud was too close by now. Less than
two hundred feet separated Rohan from the rest of the column.
The victims writhed on the ground in the intervening space as
if burning in black flames; they were probably shouting, but in
the incessant low buzz of the cloud their cries were swallowed
up, along with all other sounds, including the roar from the
forward energobot against whose force field myriad assailants
burned in a flickering blaze.

Rohan was still standing, the upper half of his body outside
the amphibian. He made no effort to take cover, not out of

desperate courage, but simply because, as he himself repeated later, he wasn't thinking about it—or indeed, about anything.

This image, which he was unable to forget—of people in a black deluge—suddenly changed in the most astounding way. The men under attack ceased writhing against boulders, running away, or crawling into the wiry scrub. Gradually they came to a stop, standing or sitting, while the cloud, dividing into a series of funnels, formed into a kind of local whirlwind over each of them, brushing in a single fluid movement against their torso or only their head, after which it moved away in a restless mass, buzzing higher and higher between the walls of the ravine till it covered the waning light of the sky; and then, in a gradually fading murmur, it slid into the rocks, dropping onto the black jungle and vanishing, such that only tiny black pinpricks scattered loosely among the now motionless figures bore witness to the reality of what had happened here a moment before.

Rohan, who still did not believe he had survived or understand why, looked around for Terner. But the cockpit was empty; the bosun must have leaped out, how or when he did not know. He saw him lying some distance away, the butts of the laser guns still pressed against his chest, staring fixedly ahead.

Rohan climbed down and ran from one man to another. They did not know him. None of them said a word. The majority seemed calm; they were lying on the rocks or sitting, while two or three of them rose to their feet, walked up to the vehicles and began touching their flanks with the slow clumsy gestures of the blind.

Rohan watched Genlis, a brilliant radar technician and friend of Jarg's, trying to move the hand grip of the transporter's

135

hatch, his mouth hanging half open, like a wild man who had never seen such a thing before.

The next moment Rohan was to understand the meaning of the round hole burned in one of the partitions on the *Condor*'s bridge. When he kneeled down and shook Ballmin's shoulders as if in this way he could bring him round, a purple flame burst with a crash right over his head. One of the men sitting farther away had taken his Weyr gun from its holster and unintentionally pulled the trigger. Rohan shouted to him, but the man paid no attention. Perhaps the flash pleased him, like a small child enjoying fireworks, because he continued to empty the nuclear magazine; the air was sizzling with heat, and Rohan, who had thrown himself to the ground, had to crawl among the boulders. At this moment there was a sudden stomping of feet and Jarg appeared from around the bend, out of breath, his face glistening with sweat. He ran directly toward the madman who was amusing himself with the Weyr. "Stop! Get down! Get down!" Rohan yelled at the top of his voice, but before the confused Jarg could stop running, he was struck by a fearful shot in the left shoulder; Rohan saw his face as his whole severed arm flew through the air, blood gushing from the ghastly wound. The man firing seemed not to notice this at all. Jarg, looking with boundless amazement first at the bleeding stump, then at the severed arm, spun around and fell to the ground.

The man with the Weyr stood up. Rohan saw how the continual fire from the ever more heated gun was sending sparks reeking of silicon smoke dancing off the boulders. The man tottered forward; his movements were exactly those of an infant carrying a rattle. The flame shot through the air between two men sitting next to each other; they didn't even close their eyes against the blinding flash. A second later and one of them would have been hit directly in the face. Rohan—once again, this was a reflex, not a decision—snatched his own Weyr from its holster and let off a single shot. The other man's bent arms snapped against his chest, his weapon clattered on the rocks, and he himself fell face down on top of it.

Rohan jumped up. Dusk was falling. Everyone needed to be taken as quickly as possible back to the base. He had only his own small amphibian: when he tried to start up one of the transporters, it turned out that two of them had collided at the narrowest point in the defile and it would have taken a crane to separate them. There remained the rear energobot, which could have taken five people at most, whereas he had nine of them—alive, though not in their right minds. He decided it would be better to gather all of them together and tie them up so they couldn't run away or do themselves any harm; he would turn on the force field of the two energobots to provide protection for them, while he himself would go for help. He chose not to take anyone with him, since the small vehicle was entirely unshielded, and in the case of attack he preferred to place only himself at risk.

Night had fallen completely by the time he finished his extraordinary task; the men allowed themselves to be tied up without resisting. He backed the rear energobot up so he could drive out in the amphibian; he set up both transmitters, turned the force field on remotely, leaving all the men tied up inside it, and set off back.

So it was that within twenty-seven days of landing on the planet, almost half the crew of the *Invincible* had been incapacitated.

DEFEAT

———

Like all true stories, Rohan's was bizarre and did not make sense. Why had the cloud not attacked him or Jarg? Why had it also not affected Terner till he left the amphibian? Why had Jarg run away, then come back? The answer to the last question was relatively easy. He'd returned, it was surmised, when he got over his panic and realized that he was thirty miles from base, a distance he could not walk with the oxygen reserves he had with him.

The other questions remained an enigma. The answers to them could mean the difference between life and death for everyone. But analyses and hypotheses had to give way to action.

Horpach learned about the fate of Rohan's team after midnight; half an hour later he lifted off.

Shifting a space cruiser from one place to another only a hundred and twenty miles away is a thankless task. The ship has to travel suspended the entire time vertically on the flames of its boosters, at a relatively low velocity, which uses up a great deal of fuel. The transmission, ill adapted for this kind of work, required the constant intervention of the electrical automatons, and even so the steel colossus moved through the night with a slight rocking, as if it were being borne on a gently swelling sea. It would no doubt have been an extraordinary sight to any observer standing on the surface of Regis III—this indistinct shape, wreathed in the light of the flames issuing from it, passing through the gloom like a column of fire.

Maintaining the correct course was no easy matter either. They had to rise above the atmosphere, then re-enter it stern first.

All of this occupied the commander's full attention, the more so because the crater they were looking for was hidden beneath a thin covering of cloud. Finally, before sunrise, the *Invincible* succeeded in landing in the crater, a mile and a half from Regnar's former base. The supercopter, the land vehicles, and the barracks were brought within the cruiser's perimeter, and a heavily armed rescue squad brought in all of the survivors from Rohan's team, in good physical shape though lethargic. Two additional cabins needed to be converted into hospital rooms, since the ship's actual sick bay had no more free places. It was only when this was done that the scientists turned to the mystery of why Rohan had been spared, along with Jarg, until the tragic incident with the mad shooter.

It was baffling, because both men were entirely indistinguishable from the others in their clothing, weaponry, and appearance. The fact that along with Terner, the three of them had been in the small amphibian craft, was surely insignificant.

At the same time Horpach was faced with the dilemma of what to do next. The situation was sufficiently clear for him to be able to return to base with information that explained the tragic end of the *Condor* and justified turning back. The things that most fascinated the scientists—the metal pseudo-insects, their symbiosis with the mechanical vegetation that grew on the cliffs, and lastly the matter of whether the cloud had a "mind"—they didn't even know if there was only one cloud or if more existed, or whether in fact smaller clouds could all merge into one homogeneous whole—none of this would have inclined him to remain on Regis III an hour longer, if it weren't the case that he was still four people short from Regnar's team, including Regnar himself.

The trail of the missing men had led Rohan's team into the ravine. Defenseless as they were, they would certainly perish there even if the inanimate inhabitants of Regis left them in peace. Thus, it was necessary to search the vicinity, because, stripped of the capacity for reasoned action, the poor fellows could only count on help from the *Invincible*.

The one thing that could be established with a reasonable degree of accuracy was the scope of the search, since the missing men, astray in the landscape of caves and ravines, could not have gone more than a couple of dozen miles from the crater. The oxygen in their tanks was low, though the physicians gave reassurances that breathing the atmosphere of the planet would definitely not be lethal, while in the present condition of those individuals, confusion brought on by high levels of methane entering the bloodstream was of course of little consequence.

The area to be searched was not so large, but the terrain was exceptionally difficult, with poor visibility. Combing all the defiles, crevices, vaults, and caves could take weeks even in favorable conditions. Beneath the rocks of the winding gullies and valleys, and linking to them only in places, there was a second, unseen network of underground passageways and chambers where water flowed. It was entirely possible that the lost men had entered such a place; in fact, it couldn't be counted on that they would all be found together. Deprived of memory, they were more vulnerable than children, because children would at least have stayed with one another. Then on top of everything else, the region was the home base of the black clouds. The powerful weapons of the *Invincible* and its technical capabilities were of little help in the search. The most reliable defense, the force field, could not be deployed at all in the channels beneath the planet's surface. The remaining alternatives, then, were to withdraw at once, which would mean a death sentence for the missing, or to commence a perilous search. This latter option had a realistic chance of success only during the following few days, up to about a week. Horpach knew that after that time, further searching could only hope to turn up the remains of the missing people.

Early the next day the commander summoned the specialists, laid out the situation and stated that he was counting on their help. They were in possession of a handful of the metallic insects that Rohan had brought back in the pocket of his tunic. Almost an entire day was devoted to examining them. Horpach wanted to know if there was a way of radically disabling these forms. The question of what had protected Jarg and Rohan from being attacked by the cloud was also revisited.

The "prisoners of war" occupied a prominent place at the council, being placed in a glass container in the middle of the table. There were only a dozen or so of them, since the others had been destroyed in the course of the examination. Each had a perfectly symmetrical tripartite shape that resembled the letter Y, with three pointed arms joined at a thicker central node, black as coal in direct light, while in indirect lighting they shimmered dark blue and dark green, like the abdomens of certain terrestrial insects that are composed of multiple tiny surfaces like the facets of a cut diamond. In their innards they contained a microscopic structure that never varied. Its components, several hundred times smaller than a grain of sand, constituted a sort of central nervous system in which semi-autonomous subsystems could be distinguished.

The smaller part, which occupied the inside of the arms of the Y, oversaw the movements of the insect, which in the microcrystalline structure of those arms possessed something along the lines of a universal rechargeable battery cum energy transformer. Depending on how the microcrystals were compressed, they formed either an electrical field or a magnetic one, or alternating force fields that could heat the central part to a relatively high temperature, at which times the accumulated heat radiated outwards unidirectionally. The movement of the air that this gave rise to, a kind of recoil, allowed the thing to rise up and move in any direction. An individual crystal didn't so much fly as drift in the air; during laboratory experiments at least it was not capable of precisely directing its own flight. Whereas when it joined with others by touching the tips of their arms together, it created an aggregate that had greater aerodynamic capabilities the more numerous it became.

Each crystal could link with three others; it was also able to attach the tip of one of its arms to the central node of another crystal, thus making possible a multilayered construction for the growing assemblages. Joining together did not have to involve actual touching, for it was enough to bring the tips close together for the magnetic field they created to hold the entire formation in equilibrium. Once it comprised a certain number of insects, the aggregate began to demonstrate numerous regularities; depending on external stimuli, it was capable of changing direction, shape, structure, frequency of internal impulses. When these altered in a particular way the poles reversed and instead of attracting, the agglomerations separated into individual crystals and scattered.

As well as a system controlling their movements, each black crystal contained a second network of connections, or rather a portion of one, for this system seemed to constitute part of some greater whole. The overarching whole, that probably arose only when a huge number of elements joined together, was the actual motor driving the actions of the cloud. At this point, however, the scientists' knowledge was exhausted. They knew nothing of capabilities of growth in the higher-level systems, and the question of their "intelligence" was especially unclear. Kronotos suspected that the tougher the problem they faced, the greater number of crystals joined together in a single whole. This sounded plausible, though neither the cyberneticians nor the computer scientists knew of any equivalent construction elsewhere, that is to say, an infinitely expandable brain that adapts its size to the magnitude of its purposes.

Some of the samples Rohan had brought were damaged. Others, though, demonstrated standard reactions. An individual one could drift about, rise almost imperceptibly, descend, approach the source of a stimulus or avoid it. Aside from this it was entirely harmless; it did not emit any kind of energy even in the face of destruction (and the scientists tried to destroy them in various ways, with chemical substances, heat, force field, and radiation); it could be annihilated like the weakest terrestrial beetle, the only difference being that its crystal-and-metal shell was not so easily crushed. Yet linked together in even a relatively small aggregation, when faced with a magnetic field the insects would begin to create their own field to neutralize the first; when exposed to high temperatures, they would attempt to shed the excess heat via infrared radiation. The experiments could not be continued as the scientists only had a handful of crystals at their disposal.

Kronotos answered the commander's questions in the name of the other head scientists. They demanded time to conduct further tests; above all, they wished to acquire a larger number of crystals. To this end they proposed sending an expedition into the heart of the ravine, which while it searched for the missing men could simultaneously collect at least several thousand samples.

Horpach consented. He decided, however, that he could no longer risk human life. He elected to send into the ravine a machine that had not thus far been utilized. It was an eighty-tonne automated special-purpose vehicle that was usually deployed only in conditions of intense radioactive contamination, or exceptionally high air pressure or temperatures. This device, commonly nicknamed the Cyclops, was kept in the bowels of the ship, held firmly in place against the bulkheads of the cargo hold. In principle it was not used on the surface of a planet, and the truth was that the *Invincible* had never once mobilized its Cyclops. Situations that called for such an eventuality, even on a scale of the entire tonnage of the space base, could be counted on the fingers of one hand. In the jargon used on board, sending out the Cyclops for some task meant the same certainty as entrusting it to the Devil himself. No one had ever heard of any Cyclops failing. The machine was lifted out with cranes and put on the ramp, where the technicians and programmers prepared it. Along with the usual system of Diracs to create a force field, it was equipped with a spherical antimatter cannon, and thus could fire antiprotons in any direction, or in all directions at once. A jet propeller built into its armored belly allowed the Cyclops to use the interference of its force field to levitate several feet above the ground, so it did not have to rely either on any surface, or on the presence of wheels or caterpillar tracks. At its front an armored maw opened up; through the aperture there extended the inhaustor, a kind of telescopic arm capable of drilling on a local scale, collecting mineral samples from outside, and managing other tasks. The Cyclops carried powerful radio and TV transmitters, but it was also adapted to independent operations thanks to a computer that steered it. The technicians of Engineer Petersen's operating team programmed the computer appropriately, as the commander expected he would lose contact with the vehicle once it was in the ravine.

The program anticipated the search for the missing men, whom the Cyclops was to take into its interior in such a way that it would first screen both them and itself with a secondary force field outside its own, and only once they were protected would it make an opening in the inner field. As well as this, the vehicle was to gather a large number of crystals from among those that would attack it. The antimatter cannon was to be employed only in extreme need, if the force field was in danger of being breached, as the effect of firing would by the very nature of things lead to radioactive contamination of the terrain that could threaten the lives of the missing men if they happened to be in the vicinity.

From end to end the Cyclops measured twenty-five feet, and was "broad in the shoulders" too—the hull was over twelve feet in diameter. If a gap in the rock blocked its way, the Cyclops could widen it either with its steel arm, or by pushing the rock aside and crushing it with the force field. But even turning off the field could not harm it, since its own ceramic and vanadium armor was hard as diamonds.

Inside the Cyclops they stowed an automaton that was to take care of the missing men once they were found; bunks were also prepared for them there. Finally, after all its equipment had been checked, the armored hull of the vehicle moved in a curiously light fashion down the lowered ramp, and as if lifted up by an invisible force—for it did not kick up dust even when it moved at top speed—it passed the blue lights indicating the opening in the *Invincible's* force field, then, watched by those gathered under the stern of the ship, it rapidly disappeared from view.

For about an hour, radio and TV communication between the Cyclops and the bridge functioned perfectly. Rohan spotted the entrance to the ravine in which the attack had taken place, recognizing it by a large obelisk like a fallen church spire that partially blocked a gap in the rocky walls. At the first point where there were large scattered boulders, the machine slowed down slightly. Its atomic drive functioned so quietly that those standing at the monitors could even hear the sound of the stream running under the rocks.

The communications specialists maintained sound and vision till 2.40, when after crossing a flat and more accessible part of the ravine, the Cyclops entered a labyrinth of rusting undergrowth. Thanks to the efforts of the radio technicians, four more messages could be sent each way, but the fifth came in so garbled that its contents could only be guessed at: The Cyclops' computer seemed to be reporting having made successful progress.

In accordance with the plan that had been agreed on, Horpach then launched a flying probe from the *Invincible*, equipped with a television relay. The probe rose steeply into the sky and vanished within a few seconds. Soon it began to transmit signals back to the ship. A picturesque landscape appeared, seen from an altitude of several miles, with innumerable jagged cliffs covered in patches of ruddy or black bushes. Within a minute they had a clear sighting of the Cyclops down below; it was moving along the bottom of the large ravine, glistening like a steel fist. Horpach, Rohan, and the heads of the specialist teams stood around the monitors on the bridge. Reception was good, but they expected it to deteriorate or break off completely, and for this reason other probes that would serve as relays were waiting to be launched. The Chief Engineer reckoned that in case of an attack contact with the Cyclops would certainly be lost, but at least it would be possible to observe its actions.

The Cyclops' electrical eyes could not see it, but thanks to the wide field of vision provided by the altitude of the teleprobe those at the monitors knew that only a few hundred yards separated the vehicle from the transporters that stood abandoned by the rock gateway, blocking the way ahead. After carrying out its other tasks, on its return journey the Cyclops was also to tow behind it the two caterpillars stuck together after the collision.

From high up, the empty transporters looked like little green boxes. By one of them a small, partially burned figure could be made out: the body of the man Rohan had shot.

Immediately before the bend beyond which stood the needles of the gateway, the Cyclops came to a halt, then approached the mane of metallic bushes stretching almost to the bottom of the ravine. They followed its movements tensely. It had to make a narrow opening in the forward part of its force field through which to extend the inhaustor. The latter—resembling an elongated cannon barrel with an knobbed fist at the end—reached out of its bushing, grasped a clump of bushes, tore it from the rocky ground without any apparent effort, then retracted, while the Cyclops backed up to the bottom of the ravine.

The whole operation had gone off smoothly. Using the teleprobe that was hovering over the ravine, they were able to make radio contact with the Cyclops' computer, which informed them that the sample, swarming with black insects, had been stowed in the hold.

The Cyclops came to within a hundred yards of the accident. The rear energobot of Rohan's team stood there, leaning its metal rump against the rock; in the gateway itself were the two transporters locked together, while beyond them was the second energobot. The faintest trembling of the air showed that its force field was still turned on, just as Rohan had left it after the attack on his unit. The Cyclops began by turning off the Diracs of the farther energobot remotely, then, increasing its thrust and rising into the air, it flew nimbly over the tilted roofs of the transporters and landed back on the rocks beyond the gateway. At that exact moment, one of the observers gave a warning shout. It rang out across the bridge of the *Invincible*, 35 miles from the ravine, in which the black scrub on the slopes began to smoke and set off in waves toward the vehicle from Earth, coming on with such vehemence that in the first instant the Cyclops disappeared completely, concealed by what looked like a cape of tarry smoke flung from above. At once, however, a ragged flash lit up the entire breadth of the attacking cloud. This was not the Cyclops using its terrible weaponry, merely the cloud's energy fields striking against the force field. It was as if the field had suddenly materialized, blanketed with a dense layer of seething black; now it swelled like an immense blister of lava, now it shrank, and this curious game went on for some time. The watchers had the impression that the machine now hidden from view was attempting to repulse a myriad assailants, whose numbers kept growing

149

and growing, as ever new clouds came streaming down the slopes toward the ravine floor. By now the glimmering sphere of the force field could no longer be seen either; the extraordinary struggle between two inanimate yet mighty forces went on in utter silence. Finally one of those standing at the monitor gave a sigh. The juddering black bubble had vanished beneath a dark funnel; the cloud had transformed into a sort of huge whirlwind that rose above the peaks of the highest cliffs and, attached at the bottom to its opponent, at the top it span at a frantic speed in a kilometer-wide maelstrom that shimmered pale blue. No one spoke; they all understood that the cloud was trying to break through the bubble of energy in which the vehicle lay like a nut in its shell.

Out of the corner of his eye, Rohan saw the commander open his mouth to ask the Chief Engineer standing next to him if the field would hold out—but the words didn't come. He didn't have time.

The black whirlwind, the walls of the ravine, the bushes—all of it disappeared in a split second. It looked as if a volcano breathing fire had opened up in a fissure in the rock. A column of smoke and frothing lava, shattered rocks, and finally, immense white billows of steam that probably came from the boiling waters of the stream, soared a mile into the air to where the TV relay was hovering. The Cyclops had activated its antimatter cannon.

None of those standing on the bridge moved an inch, no one spoke; yet at the same time none of them could suppress a sense of vengeful satisfaction. The fact that this feeling was irrational did not lessen its intensity. It seemed that the cloud had finally met a worthy adversary. All contact with the Cyclops had cut out at the moment of the attack, and from that point on the men on the bridge could only watch the images conveyed across forty miles of trembling atmosphere by the ultrashort frequency of the aerial probe. Word of the battle that had broken out in the enclosed ravine had reached those outside the bridge. Crew members who had been dismantling the aluminum barracks dropped their work. The northeastern rim of the horizon glowed as if a second sun were about to rise there, one that was brighter than the sun currently in the sky; then the glow disappeared behind a column of smoke that was forming into the shape of a bulky mushroom.

The technicians overseeing the teleprobe had to move it away from the combat; they sent it up to two and a half miles. It was only here that it got clear of the violent air currents set off by the extended explosion. There was no sign of the rocks blocking the ravine, the overgrown sides, or even the black cloud that had risen from them. The monitors were filled with tumultuous stretches of fire and smoke, crisscrossed by parabolas of burning fragments. The acoustic sensors relayed a constant rumbling, now louder, now fainter, as if a significant part of the continent had been struck by an earthquake.

The fact that the extraordinary battle kept going was astonishing. Within the space of a minute the ravine floor and the entire area around the Cyclops must have reached the temperature of incandescence; the rocks would have subsided, come tumbling down, been turned into lava, and indeed a shining crimson river could already be seen beginning to channel its way toward the entrance to the ravine, several miles from the heart of the battle. For a moment Horpach wondered if the electronic breakers of the cannon were not malfunctioning, because it seemed impossible that the cloud should continue its attack against such a devastating opponent. But when the probe was ordered even higher, ascending to the very edge of the troposphere, what appeared on the monitor showed that he was mistaken.

Now the field of vision extended to forty square kilometers. An incredible movement had begun across this ravine-scarred terrain. In what seemed like slow motion—an effect caused purely by distance—from rocky slopes hidden in patches of darkness, from hollows and caves, ever newer swirls of black were emerging, rising into the air, joining together and, consolidating in flight, were heading toward the heart of the conflict. For several minutes it might have seemed that the constant dark streams hurtling toward the fray would crush the atomic fire, but Horpach knew the energy reserves of the monster built by human hands.

The bridge was filled with a single unbroken, deafening roar from the speakers; at the same time, flames two miles high pierced the massive body of the attacking cloud and began to turn slowly, creating something like a fiery windmill; entire tracts of air quivered and bent from the heat, whose center simultaneously began to move.

For some unknown reason, the Cyclops had set off backwards and, continuing the fight at all times, was slowly reversing toward the ravine entrance. Perhaps its electronic brain had calculated that the cliffs on either side might be brought down by the atomic explosions, collapsing onto the vehicle; though it might survive even such a predicament, its freedom of movement might be impaired. In any case, the fighting Cyclops was trying to break out into more open terrain, and in the seething confusion it was no longer possible to tell what was fire from its cannon, what was smoke from the blaze, what remnants of the cloud, and what crushed rock from the crumbling pinnacles.

The cataclysm appeared to have reached its climax. The next moment, however, something quite unbelievable happened. The image was lit up by a terrible, dazzling brightness pitted by myriad explosions, and in a new burst of antimatter, the entire vicinity of the Cyclops—air, debris, steam, gases, smoke—all was transformed into maximally hard radiation that split the ravine in two, enclosed the cloud in an annihilating embrace half a mile wide, and burst into the air as if the very innards of the planet were exploding.

153

The *Invincible*, 40 miles distant from the epicenter of this ghastly strike, rocked; seismic waves moved across the desert, the transporters and energobots standing by the ramp shifted in their places, and a few minutes later a hard howling wind blew from the mountains, with an instantaneous heat seared the faces of those seeking shelter beneath the vehicles, then, stirring up a wall of spiraling sand, blew on out across the vast desert.

Some wreckage must have hit the TV probe, even though at the time it was eight miles from the center of the devastation. The connection was maintained, but the quality of the image was much worse, with a great deal of interference. A minute passed; when the smoke drifted aside somewhat, Rohan strained his eyes and witnessed the next stage in the struggle.

It was not over, despite what he had thought a moment before. If the attackers had been living beings, the massacre they had experienced would no doubt have forced subsequent waves to withdraw, or at the very least to stop at the gates of the hell that had been precipitated. But here inanimacy was fighting inanimacy. The atomic fire did not cease, it was simply that the shape and direction of the main assault changed—and it was then that Rohan understood for the first time what the conflict that had once raged across the wildernesses of Regis III must have looked like, as one group of robots pulverized and shattered another; how selection taken place in inanimate evolution; and what Lauda had meant when he said that the pseudo-insects had been victorious because they were better adapted. At the same time it crossed his mind that something like this must already have taken place here, that the billion-strong cloud, inanimate, indestructible in its crystals, and maintained by the energy of the sun, must contain knowledge of similar encounters—that it must have been with exactly such solitary opponents, heavily armored giants, atomic mammoths of the robot family, that they did battle tens of thousands of years ago, these lifeless specks that on the face of it seemed nothing next to the all-destroying firepower that could burn its way through solid rock. The thing that enabled them to survive—and caused the armor of those huge monsters to be ripped open like rusty tin cans and scattered across the great desert along with the skeletons of once precise electronic mechanisms now buried under the sand—what made this possible was an implausible, unnamable courage, if one could use such a word in relation to the little crystals of the titanic cloud. But what other word did he have for it? And despite himself, he could not avoid a feeling of admiration as he saw it continuing to act, in the face of the hecatomb that had just taken place ...

Because the cloud was continuing its attack. Now, across the entire expanse visible from the sky only the highest solitary peaks could be seen rising above its surface. Everything else, the whole landscape of ravines, had vanished beneath the deluge of black waves rushing concentrically from every direction and pouring into the depths of the fiery funnel whose center was the Cyclops, invisible beneath its shield of quaking heat. This assault, seemingly made at a cost of vast and pointless losses, was in fact not entirely futile.

Rohan, along with all those now standing helplessly on the bridge before the spectacle playing out on the monitor, was well aware of this fact. The energy reserves of the Cyclops were practically speaking inexhaustible, but the longer the constant annihilating fire was kept up, despite powerful safety devices, despite the antiradiation mirrors, a small fragment of the astral temperatures was still transferred to the cannon, returning to its source, and the interior of the vehicle would be getting hotter and hotter. That was why the attack was kept up so doggedly, why it came from every direction at once; the closer each successive clash of antimatter was to the machine's armor plating, with hails of crystals falling to their doom, the more heated all the Cyclops' systems became. For a long time now no human could have survived inside the vehicle. Its ceramite armor may well have been glowing red hot by now—though all they could see, beneath the pall of smoke, was the pale blue bulge of pulsating fire that slowly, step by step was making its way toward the entrance of the ravine, such that the location of the cloud's original attack came into view two miles to the north, revealing its hideous surface, scorched, strewn with layers of cinders and lava, with the remains of burned bushes dangling from the smashed cliffs, and filled with crystals that had been trapped there and melted into metal lumps by the thermic impact.

Horpach ordered the loudspeakers to be turned off, putting an end to the deafening roar that till now had filled the bridge. He asked Jason what would happen when the temperature inside the Cyclops exceeded the endurance of the computer.

The scientist did not hesitate for a second.

"The cannon will be deactivated."

"And the force field?"

"The force field no."

The battle had now shifted to the plain by the ravine entrance. The inky sea in the monitor frothed, swelled, churned, and plunged into the fiery maw in hellish bounds.

"It shouldn't be long now," Kronotos said in the silence of the muted confusion on the screen. Another minute passed. All at once, the flaming funnel suddenly dimmed. The cloud had covered it over.

"Thirty-five miles from us," the communications technician said in answer to a question from Horpach. The commander sounded the alarm. Everyone was ordered to their stations. The *Invincible* retracted its ramp and personnel elevator, and closed the hatches. A new flash appeared on the monitor. The burning funnel had returned. This time the cloud did not attack; only its very edges lit up, struck by fire, while the entire rest began to pull back toward the ravines, disappearing in their shadowy tangle, and the watchers saw the Cyclops, apparently unharmed. It was still reversing, very slowly, still firing constantly at everything around it—boulders, sand, dunes.

"Why isn't it turning off the cannon?" someone exclaimed. As if it had heard these words, the machine deactivated its barrage of fire, turned around, and rumbled across the desert, accelerating as it went. The flying probe accompanied it from high up. At a certain moment they saw something like a filament of fire flying at incredible velocity directly at their faces—and before they caught on that the Cyclops had fired its cannon at the probe, and that what they were seeing was the trace of particles being annihilated in the path of the shot, they flinched instinctively, stepping back as if afraid the charge would burst through the screen and explode inside the bridge. Immediately afterwards the image vanished and the screen went white.

"It shot the probe down!" shouted the technician at the control console. "Captain!"

Horpach ordered another probe to be launched. The Cyclops was so close to the *Invincible* that they saw it as soon as the probe had gained altitude. There was another thread-like flash, and it too was destroyed. Before the image disappeared, they caught a glimpse of their own ship within the probe's field of vision: The Cyclops was no more than six miles away.

"Has it gone nuts?" the other technician at the console said in a loud voice. His words unblocked something in Rohan's mind. He looked at the captain and realized they were both thinking the same thing. He felt as if his limbs, his head, his whole body had been plunged into an absurd, leaden dream. But commands were issued: Horpach ordered a third probe to be launched, then a fourth. The Cyclops shot them down one after the other, like a crack marksman amusing himself with clay pigeons.

"I need full power," said Horpach, his eyes glued to the screen.

The Chief Engineer brought both hands down on the switches of the console like a pianist striking a chord.

"Takeoff power in six minutes," he said.

"I need full power," repeated Horpach, in the same tone, and the bridge fell so silent that the buzzing of the relays behind the enamel partitions could heard, as if a swarm of bees was stirring to life.

"The core casing is too cold," began the CE. At that point Horpach turned to face him and for the third time, again without raising his voice he said:

"I need FULL power."

Without another word the engineer reached for the main breaker. In the depths of the ship the staccato bleating of the alarm signal was heard, followed by the sound of footsteps like a drumroll as everyone ran to battle stations. Horpach had turned back to the monitor. No one said anything, but now everyone understood that the impossible had happened: The commander was preparing to engage his own Cyclops in battle.

Indicators flashed and arranged themselves like troops falling into line. Five- and six-figure numbers appeared in the display of the gauge showing available power. Somewhere a cable sparked; there was the smell of ozone. In the rear part of the bridge the technicians communicated with signs, pointing to the control systems that needed to be activated.

When another probe was launched, before it was shot down it showed the Cyclops with its elongated head, crawling across rock-strewn terrain; then the screen went blank once more, filled with a silver-white glare. Any moment now the vehicle would come into direct view; the bosun of the radar operators was already stationed at the monitor of a camera that had been extended upwards from the ship's prow, thanks to which vision was enhanced. The communications technician launched yet another probe. The Cyclops seemed not to be heading directly toward the *Invincible*, which stood locked down, in full battle readiness, beneath the shield of its force field. TV probes rose at regular intervals from its bow. Rohan knew that the *Invincible* could withstand antimatter fire, but the percussion energy had to be absorbed, which would deplete its energy reserves. In this situation, the most sensible thing seemed to him to be to retreat, which is to say, take off into stationary orbit. He was expecting an order along these lines any minute now. But Horpach was silent, as if for some mysterious reason he was counting on the machine's computer coming to its senses. And indeed, as he stood there with heavy eyelids, watching the movements of the dark shape making its noiseless way through the dunes, he asked:

"Are you calling it?"

"Yes, sir. There's no answer."

"Send the signal for full shutdown."

The technicians fiddled with the controls. Streams of little lights flowed together two, three, four times beneath their hands.

"It's not responding, captain."

Why was he not taking off? Rohan couldn't understand it. Did he not want to admit defeat? Horpach! This was nonsensical! The captain shifted ... Now—now he'd give the order.

But Horpach merely took a step back.

"Dr. Kronotos?"

The cybernetician came up.

"What could they have done to it?"

Rohan was struck by Horpach's formulation, which made it sound as if he were dealing with a thinking opponent.

"The autonomous circuits run on cryotrons," said Kronotos. It was clear that what he was about to say was no more than supposition. "The temperature rose, it lost superconductivity ..."

"Do you know or are you guessing?" asked the commander.

It was a bizarre conversation, as everyone was staring straight ahead, at the monitor, which, without the need for a probe by now, showed the Cyclops moving along smoothly, though not entirely confidently, since from time to time it strayed from its course as if it were not sure where it was actually going. It fired several times at the now unnecessary probe before it hit it. They saw it fall, like a blazing flare.

"The only thing I can imagine is resonance," the cyberneti-cian said after a brief hesitation. "If their field resonated with the self-stimulating potential of the computer ..."

"What about the force field?"

"The force field doesn't screen out magnetic power."

"Too bad," remarked the commander.

The tension gradually eased, as by now the Cyclops was clearly no longer moving in the direction of its mother ship. The distance between them was beginning to increase. The machine, freed of human control, had entered the vastness of the northern desert.

"Take over from me, CE," said Horpach. "Gentlemen, let's go downstairs."

A LONG NIGHT

Rohan was woken by the cold. Barely conscious, he curled up beneath his blanket, pressing his face into the bedding. He tried to cover his face with his hands, but he increasingly felt the chill. He knew he had to wake up, but he was delaying the moment, without knowing why. All of a sudden he sat up in his bunk in the complete darkness. He felt an icy blast directly on his face. He got up and, cursing under his breath, groped for the A/C control. It had been so stuffy when he went to bed that he'd turned the dial to maximum cooling.

The air in the small cabin slowly warmed up but, half-sitting under the blanket, he was unable to get back to sleep. He looked at the luminous face of his wristwatch—it was three a.m. ship's time. Once again only three hours' sleep, he thought in irritation. The council had gone on a long time, they'd broken up around midnight. All that talking for nothing, he thought to himself. Right now, in this darkness, what would he not have given to be back at base, to not know anything about this damn Regis III, about its nightmare of inanimacy and inanimate cunning. Most of those taking part in the discussion had argued that they should take off and enter into orbit; it was only the Chief Engineer and Chief Physicist who from the beginning tended towards Horpach's position that they should stay as long as they were able to. The chances of finding the four missing men from Regnar's team were perhaps one in a hundred thousand, maybe even less. If they hadn't perished beforehand, they could have survived the atomic inferno only by moving a long distance away. Rohan would have given anything to know whether the commander wanted to stay exclusively because of them—or whether perhaps other considerations came into play. Things looked one way here, but would appear entirely differently when framed in the bald words of a report, presented in the calm light of the base, where it would have to be explained that they had lost half of their expeditionary vehicles, along with their principal weapon—the Cyclops with its antimatter cannon, that would from now on present an additional hazard for any ship landing on the planet; that the casualties included six dead, while fifty percent of the survivors were being brought back hospitalized, and would be unfit for space travel for years to come, perhaps permanently. Then, after having lost men, and vehicles, and their best equipment, they had fled—because how else could a withdrawal at this point be labeled other than as flight, plain and simple—from microscopic crystals that were the product of a desert planet, the inanimate remnants of the Lyran civilization that had overtaken that of Earth so very long ago! But was Horpach someone who took such things into account? Perhaps he himself did not fully know why he was staying put. Maybe he was counting on something? If so, what?

It was true that the biologists had suggested a possible way to defeat the inanimate insects using their own weapon. Since this species had evolved, they reasoned, its further evolution could be taken in hand. First, mutations should be introduced into large numbers of captured individuals—hereditary alterations of a particular kind that in the process of multiplying would be passed on to successive generations and would neutralize the entire race of crystals. It would have to be a very specific type of adjustment that would offer some advantage, yet at the same time would cause the new species or variety to have an Achilles' heel, a weak point that left it vulnerable. But this was precisely the kind of empty talk that came from theoreticians. They had no notion of what the mutation might actually be, how it could be introduced, how large numbers of the damn crystals could be captured, without engaging in another battle that could end in a defeat still worse than the one they'd just suffered. And even if everything came off successfully, how long would they have to wait for the new evolution to kick in? It would for sure be longer than a day, longer than a week. Then what, were they supposed to spin around Regis III like a merry-go-round for a year, two years, maybe ten? None of it made any sense. Rohan realized he'd gone too far in the other direction with the A/C: Now it was too warm again. He got up, shrugged off his blanket, washed, dressed quickly and left his cabin.

The elevator was not there. He summoned it and, as he waited in the semidarkness lit by the blinking lights of the buttons, his head weighed down by the whole burden of sleepless nights and tension-filled days, through the buzzing of blood in his temples he listened to the nighttime quiet of the ship. From time to time something rumbled in the unseen ducts; from the lower decks came the muffled sound of the idling engines, as they were still in full readiness for immediate takeoff. Dry, metallic-tasting air blew from the vertical wells at either end of the platform on which he stood. The doors slid open and he entered the elevator. He got out at eight deck. Here the passageway curved, following the outer plating of the ship; it was illuminated by a line of small blue lights. He walked on without any particular destination in mind, lifting his feet instinctively at the right places to step over the tall sills of the hermetic bulkheads, till he noticed the shadows of the team that oversaw the main reactor. Their cabin was dim, the only light coming from the dozens of gauges on the instrument panels. The men were sitting at them on folding chairs.

"They're dead," someone said. Rohan did not recognize the speaker's voice. "Want to bet? For a radius of five miles it was a thousand roentgens. They're gone. Rest assured."

"Then why are we still here?" murmured another man. Not from his voice but from where he was sitting—at the gravimeter controls—Rohan knew it was Blank, the bosun.

"Because the old man doesn't want to go back."

"Would you?"

"What else can be done?"

It was hot here, and the air was filled with the curious artificial aroma of pine needles the A/C units used to cover up the smell of the plastic piles and the armor plating, both of which heated up when the engines were running. The net result of the mingling of scents was unlike anything on any other deck of the ship. Rohan stood there, unseen by those sitting in the cabin, leaning back against the foam padding of the partition. It wasn't that he wanted to hide—he simply didn't wish to take part in their conversation.

"*He* might show up any minute," someone said after a short silence. The speaker's face appeared briefly as he leaned forward; one half was pink, the other yellow from the glow of the instrument lights with which the side of the reactor seemed to be looking down at the people huddled around its base. Like the others sitting there, Rohan immediately guessed who this referred to.

"We have the field and the radar," the bosun grunted back reluctantly.

"The field won't be much use if he comes up and fires a bilierg."

"The radar won't let him close."

"You don't need to tell me—I know him like the back of my hand."

"So what?"

"So he has antiradar. Interference systems."

"But he's all to pot. An electronic madman."

"Hell of a madman. Were you on the bridge?"

"No, I was here."

"Yeah, well I was up there. Too bad you didn't see him shooting down our probes."

"Meaning what? They deprogrammed him? That he's controlled by them now?"

Everyone's saying "them," Rohan thought to himself, they're talking as if these were living, rational beings . . .

"Proton knows. Apparently it was only the communications that got deprogrammed."

"If that's the case, why would he go for us?"

There was another silence.

"So no one knows where he is?" asked the man who had not been on the bridge.

"No. The last report came in at eleven. Kralik told me. They saw him roaming about in the desert."

"Far away?"

"You scared? Ninety miles or so from here. It'd take him under an hour. Tops."

"Maybe we've piddled around here long enough," the bosun put in irritatedly, his sharp profile showing against the colorful glimmer of lights.

Everyone fell silent. Rohan turned slowly and walked away as quietly as he had come. On the way he passed two labs. The larger one was dark, but from the smaller one light fell into the passageway through windows beneath the ceiling. He peeked inside. A group made up of only cyberneticians and physicists were sitting around a circular table—there was Jason, Kronotos, Sarner, Livin, Saurahan, and someone else whose back was turned to the others as he stood in the shadow of an oblique screen programming the great computer.

"And there are two solutions involving escalation, one of annihilation, the other of destruction. The rest is system-related," Saurahan was saying. Rohan did not cross the threshold. Once again he stood and listened in.

"The first escalating solution requires the activation of the avalanche process. A matter cannon would need to be sent into the ravine and stay there."

"One already was," someone said.

"If it doesn't have a computer, it can operate even at temperatures of over a million degrees. What's needed is a plasma cannon—plasma will stand up to anything, even on an astral scale. The cloud will behave the way it did before—it'll try to smother it, resonate with its control circuits, but there won't be any circuits, there won't be anything other than a subatomic reaction. The more matter entering the reaction, the more violent it'll be. In that way you could attract the entire necrosphere of the planet into one place and annihilate it there."

Necrosphere, thought Rohan. Oh right, the crystals are inanimate. Trust the scientists to come up with some fine-sounding new term ...

"If you ask me, the best option is the one involving self-destruction," said Jason. "But how exactly do you all envision it?"

"Well, you'd need to stimulate the formation of two large 'cloud-brains' separately, then bring them into conflict with one another. The idea would be for each cloud to recognize the other as competition in the struggle for existence."

"I get it, but how do you imagine carrying it out?"

"It's no easy task, but it's feasible if the cloud is only a pseudo-brain, and so lacks a capacity for reason ..."

"Still though, the systemic option involving a decrease in average radiation is a surer bet," said Sarner. "It'd be enough to use four hydrogen charges of fifty to a hundred megatonnes per hemisphere—less than eight hundred all told. The waters of the ocean would intensify cloud cover as they evaporated; the albedo would increase, and the sedentary symbionts would be unable to supply them with the minimum amount of energy they need to multiply."

"That calculation is based on unreliable data," protested Jason. Rohan realized a debate among specialists was brewing; he stepped back from the doorway and continued on his way.

Rather than taking the elevator, he went back to his cabin by the spiral steel ladders that normally no one used. He passed the bays of each of the higher decks in turn. In the repair shop run by de Vries's team he saw the glow of welding arcs around the motionless black figures of the arctans. From a distance he saw the round windows of the ship's sick bay, which shone with a muted violet light. A physician in a white coat moved noiselessly down the passageway, followed by a shipboard automaton carrying a set of gleaming instruments. Rohan passed dark empty mess halls, the club rooms, the library, till he finally ended up on his own deck. Outside the commander's cabin he paused in mid-stride, as though he wished to listen in on him too; but no sound came from behind the smooth door, nor the faintest glimmer of light, and the windows were tightly closed with copper-headed screws.

It was only when he returned to his cabin that he felt tired once more. His shoulders drooped; he sank heavily onto his bunk, kicked off his boots and rested his head against crossed wrists. As he sat there, by the faint glimmer of the nightlight he stared at the low ceiling, which was divided in two by a crack in the pale blue paint.

It wasn't out of a sense of duty that he had wandered around the ship, nor out of curiosity about the lives and conversations of others. He was simply afraid of the night hours, because it was then he was visited by images he preferred not to remember. Of all of them, the worst was the recollection of the man he had killed, shooting him at close range to stop him from killing others. He had to do what he did, but that did not make him feel any better. He knew that if he turned off the light he'd see the same scene again, see the other man with a faint mindless smile on his face, following the barrel of the Weyr gun swaying in his hand, stepping over the mutilated body that lay on the rocks.

The body belonged to Jarg, who had come back to die so stupidly after having miraculously survived; then a moment later the other man would fall dead, a smoking hole torn in the chest of his jump suit. He would not be able to suppress this image, which unfolded before his eyes of its own accord; he could smell the sharp stink of ozone, feel the hot recoil of the grip held in his sweaty fingers, hear the whimpering of the people that he gathered later, tying them together like a sheaf of wheat as he gasped and panted, and each time he saw them the shot man's familiar nearby face, looking as if he'd suddenly been blinded, struck him with its expression of desperate vulnerability.

There was a thud; the book he had started to read while still back at the base fell to the floor. He had put a bookmark in it, but he hadn't read a single line—there'd not been a free moment. He straightened himself on the bunk. He thought about the scientists who at that moment were devising plans to destroy the cloud, and his mouth curled in a scornful smile. It was pointless, all of it, he thought. They want to destroy ... Well, actually, so do we, we all want to destroy it, but we won't save anyone by doing so. Regis is uninhabited, humans have nothing to look for here. So where does this fury come from? After all, it's just the same as if the others had been killed by a storm or an earthquake. No one's conscious intentions, no hostile thought stood in our path. An inanimate process of self-organization ... Was it worth using all of our strength and energy to destroy it, only because to begin with we took it for a lurking enemy who first ambushed the *Condor*, then us? How many extraordinary phenomena like this, so foreign to human comprehension, might lie concealed in space? Do we need to travel everywhere bringing destructive power on our ships, so as to smash anything that runs counter to our understanding? What was the term they used—the necrosphere, which means the result of necro-evolution, the evolution of inanimate matter. Perhaps the Lyrans would have had something to say on the subject. Regis III was within range for them, maybe they were intending to colonize it after their astrophysicists foresaw that their sun was going to turn into a nova ... this may have been their last hope. If we were faced with such a situation, it goes without saying that we'd fight, we'd try to crush this black crystalline brood. But as it was ... ? A whole parsec from base, and so many light years from Earth, in the name of what exactly were we here, losing men; why were our strategists looking for the best method of annihilation, for surely there could be no question of revenge ...

If Horpach had been standing in front of him, Rohan would have told him everything. How ridiculous and at the same time how insane it was, this "conquest at any cost," this "heroic survival of humanity," this desire for retribution for the death of comrades who had perished because they were sent to that death … We were quite simply rash, we placed too much trust in our cannons and sensors, we made mistakes and now we were paying the price. It was our fault, ours alone. As he was thinking these things, in the dim light he had closed his eyes, which stung as if he had sand under his eyelids. He now understood something without words: that humankind had not elevated itself sufficiently, had not yet earned the right to that so splendidly termed stance of galactocentrism, which had long been glorified, yet which did not mean searching only for beings that resemble oneself and understanding only such beings, it meant not interfering in matters that did not concern human beings. Occupy an empty place, by all means, why not; but don't attack something that exists, that over millions of years has established its own equilibrium of survival—an active survival that is not dependent on anything except radiation forces and material forces, and that is no better and no worse than the survival of the proteinaceous compounds we call animals or human beings.

It was in precisely this state, brimming with the lofty, all-embracing galactocentric understanding of every existing form, that Rohan heard the repeated high-pitched howl of the sirens like a needle penetrating his nervous system.

Everything he had been thinking a moment before vanished, wiped away by the insistent sound filling all the decks. The next second he was out in the passageway, running with the others to the rhythm of tired footsteps, amid hot human breathing, and before he even reached the elevator he suddenly felt, not with any of his senses or even his being as a whole, but as it were through the body of the ship, of which he had become a particle, a blow that admittedly seemed immeasurably distant and indistinct, yet which ran through the hull of the cruiser from stem to stern, a blow of a force that could not be compared with anything else, and which—this too he felt—was received and parried by something even larger than the *Invincible*.

"It's him! It's him!" came shouts from among those running. They disappeared one by one into the elevators, the doors slid shut, other crew members were too impatient to wait their turn and clattered down the spiral stairs. But over the mingled voices, shouts, the bosuns' whistles, the insistent sound of the sirens, and the stamping of feet from the deck above, there came a second jolt that was soundless, yet for that very reason more powerful. The corridor lights dimmed then came back on. Rohan never imagined an elevator ride could take so long. He stood, unaware that his finger was still pressing the button with all his might, while there was only one other person in the elevator with him—the cybernetician Livin. The elevator came to a stop. As he hastened out, Rohan heard the faintest hiss imaginable, the upper registers of which were, he knew, inaudible to the human ear. It sounded like a groan coming from all the cruiser's titanium trusses at once. He reached the door to the bridge, aware now that the *Invincible* was returning fire for fire.

That, however, was basically the end of the skirmish. The looming figure of the commander stood outlined against the brightly lit monitor; the overhead lights had been turned off, perhaps deliberately, and through the bars running vertically up and down the screen and blurring the entire field of vision, it was possible to make out—seemingly immobile, its lower end touching the ground, its top immense, swelling, extending in rounded billows in every direction—the mushroom cloud from the explosion that had smashed the Cyclops to smithereens outside the triple perimeter. The air was still filled with a terrible, vitreous trembling as the detonation faded. Over it all could be heard the drone of the technician:

"Twenty thousand, six hundred at ground zero ... ninety-eight hundred at perimeter ... fourteen twenty-two inside field ..."

1420 roentgens inside the field meant that the radiation had broken through the shield, Rohan realized. He had not known such a thing was possible. But when he looked at the dial of the main power gauge, he understood what kind of charge the commander had deployed. That amount of energy would have been enough to boil the water in a medium-sized continental sea. What was there to say—Horpach had preferred not to risk coming under further fire. Perhaps he had gone too far, but now at least they were back to having only one adversary.

In the meantime, the monitors were showing an extraordinary spectacle: The curling, cauliflower-like top of the mushroom was burning with all the colors of the rainbow, from the most silvery green to deep apricot and carmine reds. Only now did Rohan notice that the desert could not be seen at all; it was concealed behind a curtain of sand that had been blown hundreds of feet into the air and hung there, shifting in a wavelike motion exactly as if it had been transformed into an actual sea. The technician continued to read the figures from the gauge:

"Nineteen thousand at ground zero ... eight six hundred at perimeter ... eleven zero two inside field ..."

The victory over the Cyclops was received in complete silence; destroying one's own device, and the most powerful one at that, was not exactly cause for celebration. People began to disperse, while the mushroom cloud continued to rise into the atmosphere; its top brightened again with another scale of colors, this time because it had been caught in the rays of the sun, which was still beyond the horizon. The cloud had already passed through the highest levels of the icy cirrus, and, far above them, it turned lilac and gold, amber and platinum; these hues passed in waves from the monitors and filled the whole bridge, which shimmered as if multicolored terrestrial flowers had been strewn over the white enamel consoles.

Rohan experienced another surprise when he saw how Horpach was dressed. He wore an overcoat—the snow-white dress coat Rohan had last seen on him during the farewell ceremony at the base. He must have grabbed the first item of clothing that came to hand. He stood there with his hands in his pockets, his gray hair sticking up, and gazed at those present.

"Mr. Rohan," he said in an unexpectedly gentle tone. "Please step into my cabin."

Rohan came up, straightening instinctively, and the commander turned around and headed for the door. They walked down the passageway one after the other; from the ventilation shafts, in the murmur of forced air there could be heard the dull, seemingly angry hum from the mass of humans filling the lower decks.

THE CONVERSATION

Rohan entered the commander's cabin; he had not been surprised by the summons. He hadn't been there often, but after his solitary return to the base in the crater he had been called on board the *Invincible* and Horpach had met with him precisely there, in his own cabin. Invitations of that kind did not usually augur well. True, at the time Rohan had been too traumatized by the disaster in the ravine to be afraid of his captain's anger. Besides, the latter had not uttered a word of reproach; he had merely questioned Rohan in great detail about the circumstances accompanying the attack by the cloud. Also present was Dr. Sax, who conjectured that Rohan had survived because he had been "stupefied," bringing about an immobility that suppressed the electrical activity of the brain so the cloud took him to have already been disabled, to be one of the wounded. As for Jarg, the neurophysiologist believed the driver had been saved by pure chance, because when he ran away he found himself beyond the compass of the attack. Terner on the other hand, who almost till the very end had tried to defend himself and others by firing his laser, had acted dutifully, but paradoxically that had been his undoing, because his brain was functioning normally and thus he attracted the attention of the cloud. The cloud was of course blind in the human sense; for it, human beings were merely some kind of mobile objects that manifested their presence by the electric potential of the cortex. The three of them—Rohan, Horpach, and Sax—had even weighed the option of protecting the humans by inducing a state of artificial stupor by administering a chemical preparation, but Sax decided that such a thing would take too long to kick in when an actual need for electrical camouflage would arise, while sending men into action in a state of stupefaction was an impossibility. In the end then, the extensive examination of Rohan had led to nothing. Rohan thought that maybe Horpach wished to pick the matter up again. He came to a stop in the middle of a cabin that was perhaps twice the size of his own. On the wall there was an intercom with a direct link to the bridge, and a row of microphones connected to the ship's internal sound system. But aside from this, there were no indications whatsoever that the commander of the ship had lived here for many years. Horpach threw off his coat. Underneath he wore pants and a loose-knit undershirt. Tufts of thick gray hair poked through the holes in the fabric on his broad chest. He sat down at an angle to the other man and rested his heavy hands on a table that was bare except for a small worn leather-bound book that Rohan did not recognize. Lifting his eyes from the commander's unfamiliar reading matter to the captain himself, he saw him as if for the first time. This was a mortally tired man who did not even try to conceal the shaking of his hand as he raised it to his forehead. Rohan realized in that instant that he did not know Horpach in the slightest, despite having served under him for four years. It had never occurred to him previously to wonder why the captain's cabin contained nothing of a personal nature, none of those trivial, often naive or amusing objects that people take into space as mementoes from childhood or from home. He felt he understood at this moment why Horpach had nothing, why on the walls there were no photographs with the faces of loved ones left behind on Earth. He had no need of anything like that because all of him was here, and Earth was not his home. Was he perhaps regretting that now, for the first time in his life? His powerful shoulders and arms did not seem old. Age showed only in the skin on his hands, which was thick, forming only reluctantly into wrinkles on his knuckles, and turning white when he straightened his fingers and studied their faint trembling with a tired, seemingly indifferent curiosity, as if he were noting something that up till now had been unknown to him. Rohan would have preferred not to see it. But the commander, inclining his head, looked him in the eye and with an almost embarrassed half-smile murmured:

"I guess I overdid it, huh?"

Rohan was stunned not so much by the commander's words as their tone, and by his whole behavior. He said nothing. He remained standing. The other man rubbed his hairy chest with a broad palm and added:

"Perhaps it was for the best."

Then a few seconds later, with a frankness he had never shown before:

"I didn't know what to do."

There was something shocking in this. At one level Rohan was aware that for several days now the captain had been as much at a loss as the rest of them; but at this moment he understood that this was not true knowledge, because at root he had trusted that the commander could see several moves ahead, more than anyone else, because it had to be that way. While now, suddenly, Horpach's nature had been revealed to him as it were doubly, because he saw his half-naked torso, his exhausted body with its unsteady hands, something that had not previously entered his consciousness, and at the same time he had heard words that confirmed the realness of his discovery.

"Sit down, young man," said the commander. Rohan sat. Horpach stood up, crossed to the washstand, splashed water on his face and neck, dried himself hurriedly and vigorously, pulled on his jacket, fastened it, and sat down opposite Rohan. With his pale blue eyes, that were always a little watery as if from facing into a strong wind, he gazed at Rohan and asked casually:

"So how are you with that … immunity of yours, or whatever? Did they look you over?"

Oh, so that's what this is about, flashed through Rohan's head. He cleared his throat.

"Yes, sir, the doctors examined me, but they didn't find anything wrong. Sax was probably correct about the stupor thing."

"Right. They didn't say anything else?"

"Not to me. But I heard … They were wondering why the cloud attacks humans only once, then leaves them to their fate."

"That's interesting. What did they have to say?"

"Lauda reckons the cloud can tell healthy people from injured ones by differences in the electrical activity of the brain. An injured person's brain has the activity of a newborn baby. Or in any case very similar. It seems that the daze I was in looks like that too. Sax thinks it might be possible to make a metal net that could be hidden in the hair, and that would send weak impulses, like the brain of an injured person. A kind of cap of invisibility. In this way a person could conceal themselves from the cloud. But it's only an idea. There's no telling if it would work. They wanted to run tests. But they don't have a large enough number of crystals—and we didn't get the ones the Cyclops was supposed to collect . . ."

"All right," sighed the commander. "That wasn't what I wanted to talk to you about . . . What we'll say now will remain between the two of us, OK?"

"OK," Rohan replied slowly, and the tension returned. The commander was not looking at him now, as if it was hard for him to begin.

"I haven't made a decision yet," he said abruptly. "Another person in my place would toss a coin. Leave . . . stay . . . But I don't want to do that. I know how often you disagree with me—"

Rohan opened his mouth, but the other man stopped him with a restrained gesture.

"No, no . . . So then, now you have your chance. I'm giving it to you. You'll make the decision. I'll do whatever you say."

He looked Rohan in the eye, then immediately closed his heavy eyelids.

"Wha . . . What do you mean, I will?" stammered Rohan. He would have expected anything but this.

"That's right, you. As we agreed, this is just between us two. You'll make the decision, and I'll carry it out. I'll answer for it at the base. Pretty reasonable conditions, don't you think?"

"Are you . . . are you serious, sir?" asked Rohan, playing for time, because he already knew it was for real.

"Yes. If I didn't know you, I'd give you longer. But I'm well aware that you go around with your own ideas . . . That you made the decision long ago. I might not have been able to drag it out of you, though. That's why you'll tell me it now, right away. Because that's an order. For this moment you'll be the commander of the *Invincible*. You don't want to say at once? Fine. You have one minute."

Horpach stood, went over to the washstand, rubbed his cheeks with his hand so hard the gray stubble could be heard beneath his fingers, and, staring into the mirror, began shaving with an electric razor as if it were the most natural thing in the world.

Rohan saw him and did not see him at the same time. His first reaction was anger toward Horpach, who had treated him so despotically, giving him the right, or actually the duty, to make a decision, binding him with his word, at the same time accepting full responsibility in advance. Rohan knew him well enough to be aware that all of this had been thought through and there was no turning back. The seconds were ticking and he would have to speak, in a moment, right away; but he knew nothing. All the arguments that he would happily have flung in his commander's face, that he had lined up like iron bricks during his nighttime meditations, had evaporated. Four men were almost certainly dead. If it weren't for the "almost," there would be nothing to weigh up, to quibble about; they would simply take off with the dawn. Now, however, that "almost" began to expand inside him. As long as he had been at Horpach's side, he had believed they ought to take off without delay. Now he felt he could never bring himself to issue such an order. He knew that that would not be the end of the Regis affair, but its beginning. It wasn't about responsibility to the base. Those four men would have continued to be present on the ship, and things would never have been the same. The crew wanted to leave. But he recalled his nocturnal wanderings and realized that after a certain time they'd begin to think about it, then they'd start talking. They'd say: "You see? He took off, leaving four men behind." And nothing else would matter. Every man had to know that the others would not abandon him, under any circumstances. That everything could be lost, but you had to have the crew on board—alive or dead. This principle did not appear in the regulations. But without it it wouldn't have been possible to fly.

"Well?" said Horpach. He put down the razor and sat facing Rohan.

Rohan moistened his lips.

"An attempt should be made . . ."

"To do what?"

"To find them . . ."

It had happened. He knew the commander would not oppose him. Actually, by now he was almost certain that this was exactly what Horpach had been counting on—that he had done it deliberately. So he wouldn't be alone in the risk being taken?

"The missing men. I understand. Very well."

"But a plan is needed. Some way, something reasonable . . ."

"We've been reasonable up till now," said Horpach. "You know how that turned out."

"Can I say something?"

"Go ahead."

"Tonight I was present at a meeting of the strategists. That is, I overheard . . . well, never mind. They're working on various ways of destroying the cloud. But surely the task is not to destroy the cloud but to find the four men. If we start up some antiproton massacre, even if any of them is still alive now there's no way they'll survive another hell of that kind. None of them. It isn't possible . . ."

"I agree," the commander replied slowly.

"You do? That's good ... So then?"

Horpach said nothing for a moment.

"Did they ... did they find any other solutions?"

"The strategists? No."

Rohan wanted to ask about something else, but he lacked the courage. The words died on his lips. Horpach looked at him as if he was expecting something. But Rohan had nothing—surely the captain didn't imagine that of his own accord, alone, he could come up with a better idea than anything proposed by all the scientists, the cyberneticians and strategists, with all their computers? That was ridiculous. Yet Horpach was regarding him patiently. They were silent. Water dripped evenly from the faucet; it was extraordinarily loud in the absolute quiet. Then, out of the silence between them, something emerged that chilled Rohan's cheeks. His whole face, his skin from neck to jaw, began to tighten as he gazed into Horpach's watery eyes, that now seemed ineffably old. By now he saw nothing aside from those eyes. He already knew.

He gave a slow nod. As if he was saying, Yes. You understand? asked the commander's eyes. I do, Rohan replied with his eyes. But as the awareness became ever clearer within him, he felt that this could not be. That no one had the right to demand this of him, not even he himself. So he continued to say nothing. He remained silent, pretending now that he did not suspect anything, that he did not know; he clung to the naive hope that since nothing had been said, what had passed between their gazes could be denied, could be dismissed mendaciously as a misunderstanding—because he realized, he felt it, that Horpach himself would never say anything to him. But the other man knew, knew everything. They sat without moving. Horpach's expression softened. It no longer conveyed expectation, nor an urgent insistence, only sympathy. As if he was saying: I understand. Very well. So be it. The commander half-closed his eyes. Another moment, and the unspoken thing would have gone away and both of them would have been able to act as if nothing whatsoever had happened. But the broken gaze made all the difference. Rohan heard his own voice.

"I'll go," he said.

Horpach breathed out heavily, but Rohan was already gripped by panic at the words he himself had uttered, and he did not notice.

"No," said Horpach. "Not like that you won't."

Rohan said nothing.

"I couldn't tell you this," continued the commander. "Or even ask for a volunteer. I have no right. But you yourself can see now that we can't just leave like that. Only a single man can go in there ... and come out again. Without helmet, vehicles, without weapons."

Rohan barely heard him.

"I'll tell you my plan. You can think it over. You can say no, because everything is still only between the two of us. This is how I imagine it: breathing apparatus made of silicon. No metal. I'll send two jeeps, unmanned, to draw the cloud, which will destroy them. In the meantime a third jeep will go there, with a person on board. That's the most risky part, because it'll be necessary to drive as close as possible, so as not to waste time on walking across the desert. There'll be enough oxygen to last eighteen hours. We have photograms of the entire ravine and the surrounding area. I believe it's best not to follow the route of the previous expeditions, but rather to drive as close as possible to the northern edge of the plateau and from there descend the cliffs into the upper part of the ravine on foot. If they're

183

anywhere at all, it will be there. There they could have survived. It's difficult terrain, there are lots of caves and potholes. If you find all of them, or any of them—"

"Exactly. How am I to get them out?" asked Rohan, feeling the prick of malicious satisfaction. At this point the plan fell apart. How casually Horpach was sacrificing him ...

"You'll have medication, something that will dope them up a little. We have something of that kind. Of course, it'll only be needed if anyone you find refuses to come voluntarily. Luckily, in their condition they can still walk."

Luckily, thought Rohan. He clenched his fists under the table, taking care that Horpach did not see. He was not at all afraid. Not yet. It was all too unreal.

"If the cloud should ... take an interest in you, you'll have to lie motionless on the ground. I thought about using some kind of drug for such an eventuality, but it would need too long to take effect. The only alternative is the head covering, the electrical simulator Sax spoke about ..."

"Have they made one already?" asked Rohan. Horpach understood the hidden meaning of the question. But he kept his cool.

"No. But it can be put together in one hour. The net is hidden in the hair. The mechanism that generates the electrical alternations will be sewn into the collar of the jump suit. All right ... you have an hour. I'd give you more time, but every hour that passes decreases the chances of saving them. As it is, the likelihood is minimal. When will you make your decision?"

"I already have."

"Don't be foolish. Are you not listening to what I'm saying? The other thing was only so you'd understand we can't leave yet ..."

"You know I'll go anyway ..."

"You won't go unless I give my permission. Don't forget that I'm still the captain around here. We're faced with a situation in which no one's ambitions count for anything."

"I get it," said Rohan. "You don't want me to feel coerced? Very well. In that case ... but what we're saying is still bound by our agreement?"

"Yes."

"In that case I'd like to know what you would do in my position. Let's switch places—the opposite to a moment ago."

Horpach was silent for a moment.

"What if I told you I would not go?"

"Then I won't either. But I know you'll tell me the truth ..."

"Then you won't go? Word of honor? No, no ... I know that isn't necessary ..."

The commander stood. Rohan rose to his feet too.

"You didn't answer me, sir."

The commander studied him. Horpach was taller, altogether bigger and broader in the shoulders. His eyes took on the same weary expression as at the beginning of the conversation.

"You can go," he said. Rohan straightened without thinking and walked toward the door. The commander made a gesture as if he wished to keep him back, place a hand on his shoulder, but Rohan didn't notice. He left; Horpach remained motionless by the door as it closed, and stood there for a long time.

INVINCIBLE

The first two jeeps rumbled down the ramp at dawn. The curving dunes that faced the sun were still black with the darkness of night. The force field opened up, letting the vehicles through, then closed again in a flicker of blue lights. By the stern of the ship Rohan crouched on the rear step of the third jeep, dressed in a jump suit, with no helmet or protective goggles, only a small oxygen mask over his mouth. His hands were clasping his knees, fingers interwoven, because in this position it was easier for him to watch the twitching second hand of his watch.

In the top left pocket of the suit he had four ampoules for the injections; in the right-hand pocket were flattened tablets with nutritional concentrate, while the thigh pockets were stuffed with various small instruments: a Geiger counter, a small magnetic sensor, a compass, and a microphotogram map of the terrain, no larger than a postage stamp, which had to be read with the aid of a powerful magnifying glass. Thin plastic rope was wound six times around his waist, and practically his entire clothing was devoid of metal parts. He couldn't even feel the net of fine wires hidden in his hair, unless he consciously moved his scalp; nor did he sense the current circulating in it, though he could control the signal sent by the microtransmitter sewn into his collar with pressure from his finger: The tiny hard cylinder made a regular ticking sound, and its pulse could be felt by hand.

To the east there was a hazy red line in the sky, and the wind was already stirring, whipping up the sandy tops of the dunes. The jagged edge of the crater that constituted the horizon there seemed to be gradually melting in the swelling redness. Rohan raised his head; he was to be deprived of two-way radio contact with the ship, because an operational transmitter would have immediately betrayed his presence. But in his ear he had a tiny receiver no bigger than a cherry stone, which meant that from time to time at least, the *Invincible* could send him a message. At the present moment the receiver spoke, and it was almost as if a voice had sounded inside his head:

"Attention, Rohan. This is Horpach ... The prow sensors have detected an increase in magnetic activity. The other jeeps are probably under the cloud ... I'm sending up a probe."

Rohan looked into the brightening sky. He did not see the rocket actually take off; it suddenly shot into the sky like a firework, trailing a narrow stream of white smoke that swathed the ship's prow, then it hurtled northeast at a dizzy speed. Minutes passed. The swollen disk of the sun was already perched on the rim of the crater as if straddling it.

"A small cloud is attacking jeep number one," came the voice in his head. "Number two is moving forward unhindered so far ... Number one is approaching the gateway in the rock ... Attention! We just lost control of number one. Visual contact too—it's hidden behind the cloud. Number two is coming up to the bend by the seventh defile ... it is not being attacked ... It's started! We've lost control of jeep number two. They're all over it ... Rohan! Attention! Your jeep will be departing in fifteen seconds. After that it's over to you. Turning on the starter mechanism. All the best ..."

Horpach's voice went away abruptly. It was replaced with a mechanical ticking counting the seconds. Rohan settled himself, braced his feet, slipped one arm around the electrical loop fastened to the upper guard rail on the jeep. The light vehicle suddenly trembled, then moved forward smoothly. Horpach had kept all personnel inside the ship. Rohan was almost grateful for this; he could not have handled any farewells. In this way, clinging to the step of the bouncing jeep, all he could see was the huge, slowly receding pillar that was the *Invincible*; the blue glow that a moment before had glimmered on the flanks of the dunes told him that the vehicle was passing the boundary of the force field. Immediately afterwards the pace picked up, and ruddy billows of dust thrown up by the balloon tires blocked his view; he could barely see the dawning sky above. It was not a particularly advantageous position—he could be attacked at any time without seeing it coming. For this reason, instead of staying put as planned, he turned around, rose to his feet and, holding on to the rail, stood on the step. Thanks to this, he was now able to see over the flat top of the unmanned vehicle and watch the desert rushing toward him. The jeep was moving at maximum speed, jolting and bouncing at times, forcing Rohan to press against its surface with all his strength. The engine was barely audible; he heard only the wind whistling past his head, while grains of sand got in his eyes, and plumes of sand rose on either side, blocking the view. Before he knew it he was out of the crater. The jeep must have slipped through one of the sandy gaps in the northern rim.

All at once Rohan heard a singsong signal drawing closer. It was the transmitter of the TV probe that had been sent so high up he couldn't see it in the sky, however hard he peered. It had to be way up there so as to avoid attracting the attention of the cloud, though at the same time its presence was crucial— otherwise the ship would not have been able to control the jeep. An odometer had been specially mounted on the rear of the vehicle to help Rohan get his bearings. He'd traveled twelve miles so far, and any moment now he could expect to reach the first of the cliffs. But the low disk of the sun, which up to this point he had had on his right side, its red scarcely visible through the billowing dust, now shifted a little to the rear. This meant the jeep had swung to the left; Rohan tried in vain to figure out if this change of direction matched the previously agreed-upon route, or whether it was making it longer; the latter would mean that on the bridge they'd spotted some unexpected maneuver on the part of the cloud and were trying to move him away from it. A moment later the sun vanished behind the first sloping ridge of rock. Then it reappeared. In the slanting light the landscape looked desolate, and it did not resemble the place Rohan remembered from his previous expedition. Though then he had been observing it from higher up, from the turret of the transporter. All at once the jeep began to lurch from side to side so roughly that he kept knocking his chest painfully against the plating. He had to strain every muscle to avoid being thrown off his narrow perch by the bumps, which were not softened even by the balloon tires. The wheels danced over the rocks, in places spinning furiously, in others flinging up loose gravel that then tumbled noisily down the slope. Rohan felt as if this infernal advance must have been noticeable for miles around, and began seriously wondering if he shouldn't stop the jeep—just below his shoulder was the jutting lever of a brake that had been fixed on the outside of the vehicle—and continue without it. But then he'd be faced with a journey of many miles on foot, reducing his already slim chances of reaching his destination in a timely manner. So then, gritting his teeth, his hands desperately clamped around the grips that no longer seemed as firm as before, he continued to stare over the vehicle's flat roof toward the top of the slope. The hum of the radio probe faded from time to time, but it must still have been in the sky above him, because the jeep was maneuvering effectively, dodging piles of rock debris; every so often it would tilt to one side, slow down, then resume full speed uphill.

The odometer showed he had gone 16 miles. The route had measured 35 on the map, though it was certainly going to be longer, if only because of the endless zigzags and turns. Now there was no trace of sand; the sun, huge and practically devoid of warmth, hung ponderous and seemingly ominous, its edge still touching the jagged rock ridges. The jeep, tossed by frenetic convulsions, sped inexorably across the scree, occasionally sliding downward along with the grinding lava, its tires whining as they spun helplessly against rocks on an increasingly steep incline. 17 miles; he could hear nothing except the buzzing of the probe signal. The *Invincible* was silent; why? He had the impression that the cliff-edge whose hazy blackish outline he could make out against the red sun was the upper rim of the ravine he needed to descend into, only not here but much higher up, from the north. 18 miles. In any case, he was not seeing any sign of the black cloud. It must already have dealt with the other two jeeps. Had it simply abandoned them, satisfied with having cut them off from the ship by blocking radio contact? His own jeep was tossing like an animal in distress; at times the juddering of the engine working at full throttle grew unbearable. The vehicle's speed kept dropping, but even so it was making amazingly good progress. Maybe a hovercraft would have been even better? But the hovercraft was too large and cumbersome, and besides, it wasn't worth thinking about, since it was too late now to change anything.

He tried to look at his watch, but he was unable to—he couldn't bring his hand up to his face even for a second. He tried to flex his knees so as to soften the terrible bumps that were turning his innards upside down. All at once the front of the jeep reared up and it lurched downwards and to the side; the brakes squealed, but loose rock was being flung up on every side, drumming against the thin armor plating; the vehicle skidded, spun uncontrollably, for a moment went sideways down the river of rocks, then came to a standstill.

Slowly it turned about and set off stubbornly back up the slope. Now he could already see the ravine. He recognized it from the black patches of hideous undergrowth covering its steep sides like mountain scrub. He was perhaps half a mile from the rim of the ravine. 21 miles . . .

The slope he still had to climb looked like an unbroken sea of scattered rubble. It seemed impossible that the jeep would find a way through. He'd stopped looking for possible routes, since he had no way of controlling the vehicle's movements anyway. Instead, he tried to keep sight of the rocks circling the ravine. At any moment the black cloud could emerge from there.

"Rohan . . . Rohan . . . ," he heard suddenly. His heart beat faster. He recognized Horpach's voice.

"The jeep will probably not be able to take you all the way. From here we can't estimate the angle of the incline with sufficient accuracy, but it looks like you only have another three or four miles of navigable terrain. When the jeep can't go any further, you'll have to continue on foot. I repeat ..." Horpach reiterated the message. 25 miles or so at best ... I'll have about ten more still ahead of me, which in these conditions means at least four hours if not more, Rohan quickly calculated. But maybe they're wrong, maybe the jeep will make it through ...

The voice fell silent, and once again all that could be heard was the rhythmical, melodic buzz of the probe. Rohan bit on the mouthpiece of the mask, because the jolting caused it to rub against the inside of his lips. The sun was no longer touching the nearest mountain, but neither was it climbing into the sky. Before him he could see larger and smaller boulders and rock faces; at moments he found himself within their cool shadow. His vehicle was moving a lot more slowly now. When he raised his eyes he could see faint puffy white clouds breaking apart in the sky. Several stars were visible. All at once, something strange happened with the jeep. Its back end dropped, the front rose into the air and for a second it staggered like a horse standing on its hind legs ... one more moment and it would have come crashing over backwards, pinning Rohan underneath it, if he hadn't quickly jumped off. He landed on his hands and knees, feeling the painful impact through his thick gauntlets and knee pads; he skidded two yards or so down the scree before finally coming to rest. The jeep's wheels whined one final time, then the whole thing stopped moving.

"Attention, Rohan ... You're at mile 24 ... The jeep can't go any further. You'll need to continue on foot. Use the map. The jeep will remain where it is—if you're unable to return any other way, your coordinates are 46 by 192 ..."

Rohan slowly rose to his feet. Every muscle in his body ached. But it was only the first steps that hurt; he soon got into his stride. He was anxious to get as far as possible from the jeep, which had come to a halt between two sills of rock. He sat down under a huge obelisk, took the map out of his pocket and tried to read it. It was not easy. Finally he managed to figure out his location. He was about half a mile from the rim of the ravine as the crow flies, but at this point he couldn't even think of descending into it—the sides were uniformly blanketed with metal undergrowth. So he went uphill, continually asking himself whether he should try and get to the bottom of the ravine earlier than the spot that had been picked out. That place was going to take him at least four hours to reach. Even if he were able to return by jeep, he'd have to reckon with a return journey of five hours, and how much time would the descent itself take, not to even mention the search? All at once the entire plan seemed to make no sense whatsoever. It was nothing more than a gesture as pointless as it was heroic, by which Horpach was sacrificing him to ease his own conscience. For a while he was so overcome with rage—he'd been played like a little kid, Horpach had planned this all along—that he barely saw what was around him. Bit by bit he calmed down. There's no retreat, he kept repeating to himself, I'll do what I can. If I don't make it down into the ravine, if I don't find anyone by three o'clock, I'm heading back. It was fifteen after seven. He tried to take long even strides, though not too quickly, because oxygen use increased dramatically with greater exertion. He fastened the compass to his right wrist so he would keep to the right direction. Several times, though, he had to skirt crevasses with vertical sides. Gravity on Regis was a lot weaker than on Earth, and that at least gave a relative freedom of movement even in such rugged terrain. The sun had risen into the sky. Rohan's hearing, which was accustomed to the permanent accompaniment of sounds that had surrounded him like a sheltering barrier on his previous expeditions by vehicle, now felt naked and sharpened. He only heard from time to time the rhythmic singing of the probe, much fainter than before; but every gust of wind against the rock ridges set him on edge, because in it he thought he heard the low buzzing that he knew and remembered so well. He gradually got into his stride, and this freed up his thinking as he stepped instinctively from one rock to the next. In his pocket he had a pedometer; he was reluctant to check it too soon, and had decided to do so only after an hour. But he couldn't help himself, and took the little watchlike device out before the time was up. It proved a painful disappointment: He hadn't even gone two miles. He must have gained too much altitude, and that had slowed his progress. So it wasn't going to be three or even four hours, but another six at least, he thought to himself. He took out his map and, kneeling on the ground, lined it up a second time. The upper rim of the ravine could be seen seven or eight hundred yards to the east; he had been walking more or less parallel to it the whole time. In one place the black undergrowth on the slope was broken by a narrow, winding gap, probably the bed of a dried stream. He stared at the place. On his knees, the gusty wind whistling over his head, he hesitated for a moment. As if without knowing yet what he would do, he stood up, slipped the map automatically into his pocket, and set off at a right angle to his previous route, heading for the cliffs of the ravine.

He moved toward the silent, jagged rocks as if at any moment the ground might open up beneath his feet. A ghastly fear gripped his heart. Yet he kept walking, still swinging his arms, which were terrifyingly empty. He stopped suddenly and looked into the valleys, toward the desert where the *Invincible* stood. He couldn't see it as the ship was over the skyline. He

195

knew that, yet still he stared at the sky, ruddy along the horizon, and slowly filling with billowing white clouds. The sound of the probe had become so faint he wasn't sure whether it was an illusion. Why was the *Invincible* not saying anything?

Because it doesn't have anything else to say to you, he answered himself. The uppermost rocks of the ravine walls, which resembled grotesque sculpted figures eaten away by erosion, were close at hand. The ravine itself opened up before him like a huge trench plunged in darkness—the rays of the sun had not yet penetrated even half way down the black-covered sides. Here and there, white needles looking like limestone poked out from the bristling jungle. In a single glance he took in the entire vast space, all the way to the rocky bottom a mile away in a vertical line, and he suddenly felt so exposed, so vulnerable, that he knelt instinctively so as to cling to the rocks and become like one of them. It was a needless gesture, for he was in no danger of being noticed. The thing he needed to be afraid of had no eyes. He lay on a gently warmed slab of rock and looked downward. The photogrammetric map offered an entirely useless truth, because it showed the terrain from a bird's eye view, in appalling vertical shorthand. It was out of the question to descend via the narrow bare strip between two banks of black bushes. It would have required not twenty-five yards of rope but a hundred at least, plus he'd need pitons and a mallet, and he had nothing of the sort, he was not equipped for rock climbing. To begin with, the slim gully was not too steep, then at some point it dropped away, vanishing from view behind an overhang in the ravine wall, then reappeared far below in a blueish haze. An idiotic thought occurred to him—if only he had a parachute ...

He stared doggedly at the slopes on either side of the place where he lay pressed against a large mushroom-shaped boulder. It was only now that he felt a gentle stream of heated air flowing from the great chasm open before him. In fact, the opposite slope was trembling slightly. The jungle was a storage battery for solar rays. As his gaze moved toward the southwest, he spotted the tops of the pinnacles whose base formed the rock gateway where the disaster had occurred. He would not have recognized them if it hadn't been for the fact that, in contrast to all the other rocks, they were completely black, and glistened as if coated with a thick glaze—their upper strata must have boiled during the battle between the Cyclops and the cloud. But from his position he couldn't see the transporters, or even any signs of the atomic explosion on the floor of the ravine. He lay there and was suddenly overcome with despair: He had to go down there, to the bottom, and there was no path. Instead of relief that in this way he could go back and tell the commander he'd done everything he could, he felt a sudden burst of determination.

197

He stood up. Out of the corner of his eye he caught sight of some movement far down in the ravine, and dropped to the boulder once again, but straightened up at once. If I'm going to be throwing myself down flat every two minutes I won't get a whole lot done, he thought. He walked along the edge of the cliff, looking for a way down; every couple of hundred yards he leaned over the chasm and saw the same unchanging sight—where the slope was less steep it was covered with black bushes, whereas in the places where they did not grow, the sides dropped away vertically. At one moment he accidentally kicked a rock that went rolling downward. It brought other rocks with it, and the little landslide clattered downhill and crashed into a shaggy rock face a hundred yards or so below him. A slender skein of smoke rose from the place and glittered in the light; it spread out in the air and hung immobile for a moment as if taking a look. Rohan froze. A long minute later the skein thinned out and was noiselessly reabsorbed into the glistening bushes.

It was almost nine when, looking from behind yet another boulder, down below, at the very bottom of the ravine—which at this point was considerably wider—he noticed a bright, indistinct object that was moving. With a trembling hand he took a small pair of folding binoculars from his pocket and trained them on the place.

It was a person. The magnification was too small to make out his face—but he could see the perfectly even movements of his legs. He was walking slowly, with a slight limp, as if dragging an injured foot. Should Rohan shout to him? He was afraid to. He did try; but his voice refused to come out. He hated himself for that damned fear. He knew for sure now, though, that he would not turn back. He made a note of where the other man had been—he was moving uphill in a broadening valley, heading toward the whitish cones of scree—and he set off running in the same direction along the clifftop, leaping over boulders and crevasses, till he began to choke as his breath rasped in the mouthpiece and his heart started thumping in his chest. This is madness, I can't keep this up, he thought to himself, not knowing what to do next. He slowed down, and at that exact moment an inviting gully opened before him. Lower down it was bordered on both sides by black undergrowth, then the slope fell away; was there an overhang there?

His watch made the decision for him: It was almost half past nine. He started to climb down, initially facing the chasm, then, when the going got too steep, he turned and descended backwards, step by step, helping himself with his hands; the black bushes were close, they seemed to burn with a silent, still heat. His temples were pounding. He stopped on a rock ledge that led diagonally downward, jammed his boot between it and another ledge, and peered down. About forty yards below he could see a broad shelf from which a distinct crest of rock that rose higher than the bristling black jungle led toward the ravine floor. But empty air separated him from the shelf. He looked back—he'd come down a good two hundred yards, maybe more. The thud of his heart seemed to make the air vibrate. He blinked over and over. Slowly, gropingly, he began to unwind the rope. Surely you're not going to do anything so crazy, a voice inside him said. Moving downhill sideways, he reached the nearest bush. Its sharp outgrowths were covered with a deposit of rust that sent up puffs of dust when touched. He took hold of it, expecting who knows what, but nothing happened. He heard only a dry, creaky rustle. He tugged harder; the bush stood firm. He looped the rope around its base, tugged again … In an onrush of boldness he wrapped the rope around the bases of a second and third bush, braced himself, and pulled as hard as he could. They held fast, rooted in a cracked boulder. He began to let himself down; to begin with he was able to transfer part of his body weight to the rock using the friction provided by the soles of his boots, but all at once he slipped and found himself suspended in midair. He let the rope out ever more quickly from under his knee, holding it back with his right arm, until, watching carefully downward the whole time, he landed on the shelf. Now he tried to release the rope, pulling at its end. The bushes would not release it. He yanked it a few times. It was stuck. So he sat down straddling the rock and pulled with his entire weight, till with a vicious shush the rope came tumbling through the air and smacked him on the back of the neck. He shuddered. He remained sitting for a few minutes, his legs too wobbly to risk continuing his journey. But he did see the figure walking down below. It was a little larger. It seemed strange to him that it was such a light color; and there was also something curious about the shape of the man's head, or rather his headgear.

He would have been mistaken to think the worst was behind him. Though the truth was, such a thought did not occur to him. But he did have a hope that turned out to be false. The way ahead was much easier technically speaking, but it was lifeless; the bushes covered in gritty rust disappeared and were replaced by others that seemed to glisten with a greasy blackness, with wiry whirls dotted with the fruitlike nodes that he recognized at once.

From time to time little puffs of smoke rose from them with a faint buzz and hovered in the air. At such moments he froze—not for too long, as he would never have made it to the bottom of the ravine. For some time he straddled the rock as if he were on a horse, then the crest widened and grew less steep, and he was able to walk on it, not without difficulty, not without using his hands, but he was barely conscious of his actions on that long descent, his attention fully focused on what was on either side of him. At times he had to pass so close to the dense bushes that their bristly wires brushed against the folds of his jump suit. Yet not once did the little clouds approach him from where they hung in the air, glittering in the light. When he finally stood on the scree-covered slope, only a few hundred yards from the ravine floor with its bone-dry white boulders, it was almost twelve o'clock. By now he was below the line of the black bushes; the hillside he'd come down was half lit by the sun, which stood high in the sky. Now he could estimate the distance he'd come. But he didn't so much as glance backward. He ran downhill, striving to shift his weight from one foot to the other and one rock to another as quickly as possible, but even so the vast mass of loose scree began sliding down along with him with a grinding sound, clattering ever louder; then, very close to the dried-up stream bed, the loose rock abruptly skidded from under his feet. The impact of the fall dislodged his oxygen mask, and he rolled a dozen yards or more down the slope. He was about to leap up again and set off running, with no care for his injuries, because he was afraid the man he'd seen from the clifftop would disappear from view—both sides of the ravine, especially the opposite wall, were riddled with the black openings of caves—when something warned him, and before he was conscious of what he was doing he threw himself back down onto the sharp rocks and lay there, arms outspread. A shadow cast from high up fell over him; amid a growing hum, which increased evenly, encompassing every point on the scale from a high hiss to bass notes, he was surrounded by a black, shapeless mass. Perhaps he should have closed his eyes, but he didn't. His last thought was the hope that the device sewn into his suit had not been damaged by the fall. Then he sank into a state of inertia that he may well have deliberately imposed on himself. He didn't even move his eyeballs, yet he saw the swirling cloud hover over him, saw it send down a languid limb, the tip of which was visible up close—it looked like the mouth of an inky-black glistening whirlwind.

With his scalp, the skin of his cheeks, his whole face, he felt the tepid touch of the air, like a breath broken down into myriad tiny particles. Something grazed the breast of his suit, he was plunged in almost total shade. All at once the limb, continually twisting like a miniature tornado, withdrew into the cloud. The buzzing sound intensified. It set his teeth on edge, he could feel it inside his skull. It faded. The cloud moved upward almost vertically, became a black mist stretching from one valley wall to the other, split into separate clumps each spinning around its own axis, dropped into the motionless fuzz of the undergrowth and vanished. For a long while he lay still, as if dead. It occurred to him that perhaps it had already happened. That maybe he would no longer know who he was, how he had gotten there, nor what he should do next, and the thought terrified him so much that he sat up with a jolt. He felt like laughing. If he could think those thoughts, it meant he'd survived. That the cloud had not harmed him. That he'd fooled it. He tried to suppress the idiotic, tickling laugh that was gathering in his throat and starting to make him shake all over. It's just hysteria, he thought, rising to his feet. He was almost completely calm already, or so it seemed to him at least. He straightened his oxygen mask and looked around. The person he'd seen from the ridge was nowhere in sight. But he could hear his steps. The other man must have passed this place and vanished behind a fallen boulder that blocked half the ravine floor. He ran after him. The sound of the steps was close and strangely loud. It was as if the other man were wearing iron boots. He ran, feeling stabs of pain in his shin from ankle to knee. I must have twisted my foot, he thought, swinging his arms desperately. Once again he was short of breath, he was virtually choking. Then he saw the other person. He was walking in a straight line with long mechanical strides, stepping from rock to rock. The white cliff face threw back the sound with a clapping echo. All at once, Rohan's heart sank. It wasn't a human being, it was a robot. One of the arctans. He hadn't even given a thought to them, to what could have happened to them after the disaster; they had been in the middle transporter when the cloud attacked. It was only a few dozen yards away. At that moment he saw that the robot's left arm hung shattered and useless, while its once shiny convex plating was scratched and dented. He was hugely disappointed, yet at the same time somewhat cheered that he'd at least have this companion as his search continued. He was about to shout to the robot, but something held him back; he merely quickened his pace, passed it, and waited in his path; but the seven-foot giant didn't so much as notice him. From close up Rohan could see that part of its radar antenna, a little like a bowl-shaped ear, was smashed, and where the lens of its left eye had been there was a gaping hole with jagged edges. All the same, the robot was walking entirely steadily on its huge feet, though the left one trailed a little. Rohan called to it when they were only a few steps from one another, but the machine continued moving directly toward him as if it were blind, and at the last minute he had to jump out of its way. He ran up to the robot a second time and tried to grab its metal hand, but the robot pulled away with a smooth indifferent gesture and strode on. Rohan realized that the arctan too was a victim of the attack and could not be counted on. Yet for some reason he found it difficult to abandon the helpless device to its fate, and besides, he was curious to know where in fact it was going, because as it walked it chose the most even path possible, as if it had a particular destination in mind. After a brief moment of reflection, during which the robot moved ten or fifteen yards further on, Rohan eventually set off after it. The robot reached the bottom of a slope of loose rock and began to climb, blithely ignoring the stream of rubble sent rolling downhill by its broad feet. It clambered to perhaps half way up the slope, then all of a sudden fell over, slid downwards, its feet still moving in the air, which in other circumstances might have made a spectator laugh. Then it got up and began its ascent once more. Rohan turned around swiftly and walked away, but for a long time he continued to hear the clatter from the slope and the repeated ponderous footsteps, which the cliff walls kept sending back in multiple echoes. Now Rohan was moving rapidly, since the route along the flat rocks lining the stream bed was relatively smooth and led gently downward. There was no sign of the cloud; only a barely perceptible trembling in the air over the sides of the ravine signaled the activity seething in the black undergrowth. In this way he reached the broadest part of the ravine, which here turned into a valley surrounded by rocky inclines. About a mile and a half further on was the gateway in the rock that had been the site of the disaster. It was only now that he felt the want of an olfactory sensor to be able to seek out a human trail; but the apparatus was too cumbersome to be carried on foot. He had to manage without. He stopped and let his gaze move slowly along the cliffs. That anyone should have survived by sheltering in the metal jungle was out of the question. There remained only caves, caverns, and hollows in the rock, of which he could see four from where he stood. Their insides were hidden from view by tall thresholds with vertical sides that promised an arduous climb. For this reason he decided to look in the caves one by one. Earlier, while still on board the ship, he had spoken with the doctors and psychologists about where the missing men should be looked for, which is to say, where they might have taken refuge. But the discussions had not been especially helpful, since the behavior of those suffering from amnesia was unpredictable. The fact that the four missing men had moved away from the rest of Regnar's team indicated that they were active, unlike the others; to some extent, too, the circumstance that up to the point Rohan had reached, the four sets of tracks all led in the same direction permitted the hope that the men might all be found together. Assuming, of course, that they were still alive, and that they hadn't gone their separate ways beyond the gateway. One by one, Rohan checked out two small caves and four larger ones whose entrances were fairly easy to reach, requiring only a few minutes of untroublesome ascent via a series of large slabs of rock arranged diagonally up the slope. In the last of the caves he came across some metal remains partially submerged in water; at first he took them to be the skeleton of the second arctan, but the remains were immensely old and did not resemble any construction he was familiar with. In a shallow pool visible in the faint daylight reflecting off the smooth, polished-looking ceiling, there lay a most bizarre elongated form a little like a sixteen foot long cross; the plating that had covered it on the exterior had long since fallen apart, and now formed a rust-red mulch mingled with mud at the bottom of the pool. Rohan could not allow himself much time to examine this extraordinary find, which may have been the ruins of one of the macro-robots destroyed by the victorious cloud during the inanimate evolution. He merely made a mental note of its shape, including the loosened outlines of some fastenings and rods that looked like they served for flying rather than walking. But his watch urged haste, and so without further ado he set about searching more caves. There were so many of them, often

205

visible from the valley floor like black windows in the tall rock walls; the passages and underground galleries, often filled with water, some of which led to vertical wells and sumps with icy, roaring streams of water, were so twisting that he did not dare go deeper into them. Plus, he had nothing but a small flashlight with a weak beam that was particularly useless in extensive caves with high ceilings and multiple stories—he found several like this. Finally, almost collapsing from weariness, he sat on a large flat sun-warmed rock at the entrance to a cave he'd just searched, and chewed on an energy tablet, washing the dry substance down with water from the stream. A few times he thought he heard the buzz of an approaching cloud, but it must only have been the sound of the Sisyphean efforts of the arctan in the upper reaches of the valley. He felt a lot better after he'd eaten his meager rations. The strangest thing for him himself was that he was actually less and less bothered by the dangers surrounding him—for the black bushes stretched up every slope his gaze encountered.

He climbed down from the high place in front of the cave where he'd rested, and at that moment spotted something like a thin rusty streak on the dry boulders across the stream. When he drew closer, he saw it was traces of blood. They were completely dry, and had changed color; if it hadn't been for the exceptional whiteness of the rock, which was as bright as lime-stone, he would certainly not have noticed them. For a moment he tried to figure out which direction the bleeding person had been going, but it was impossible to tell. So he set off randomly up the valley, reasoning that this may have been someone injured during the Cyclops' battle with the cloud, and escaping from the fray. The traces crisscrossed, in some places disappeared, but eventually led him close to a cave he had searched right at the beginning. His surprise was all the greater when it turned out that by the cave entrance there was a narrow vertical shaft like a well that he had overlooked before. The trail of blood led here. Rohan knelt and leaned over the half-dark opening, and though he was prepared for the worst, he could not suppress a stifled cry, for he found himself looking at the head of Bennigsen staring back at him with empty eye sockets and bared teeth. He recognized him from his gold-rimmed spectacles, whose lenses had survived through an irony of blind chance, and now glinted clearly in the light that reflected off the limestone slab overhanging the rocky tomb. The geologist was dangling between two boulders; his body had remained vertical, trapped by the shoulders in the natural walls of the pothole. Rohan did not wish to leave human remains in such a position, but when, steeling himself, he attempted to lift the corpse, he felt it soften in his grip beneath the thick fabric of the jump suit. Decomposition had done its work, hastened by the action of the sun, which reached this place every day. Rohan merely opened the zipper of the breast pocket and took out the scientist's ID tag. Before he left, using all the strength he had he shifted one of the nearby rock slabs to cover the grave.

Rohan had found his first man. Once he had left the place it occurred to him that he really ought to have measured the body for radioactivity, since to some extent its level could have shed light on what had happened to Bennigsen himself and the others: A significant increase in radioactive levels would have shown that the dead man had been close to the atomic clash. But he'd forgotten to do so, and now nothing would have induced him to remove the tombstone again. At the same time Rohan realized the great role played in his search by chance, for he thought he had combed the place thoroughly before.

Driven by a new idea, he now hurried off following the trail of blood, seeking its beginning. It led in an almost completely straight line down the valley, as if headed toward the atomic battleground. But after a few hundred yards it turned sharply to the side. The geologist had lost a huge amount of blood, which made it all the most astonishing he had made it as far as he did. The rocks, which had not seen a drop of rain since the accident, were liberally spattered. Rohan clambered up the large, unstable boulders and found himself in a broad channel-like depression beneath a bare fin of rock. The first thing he saw was the unnaturally large metal sole of a robot's foot. It lay on its side, broken almost in two by what must have been a burst of fire from a Weyr. A little further off, leaning against a boulder, a man was half-sitting, bent almost double, wearing a helmet whose dome was black from soot. He was dead. The gun still hung from his unclenched hand, its shining muzzle resting on the ground. To begin with, Rohan lacked the courage to touch the man, only kneeling to try and see his face, but it was as distorted by decay as Bennigsen's. All at once he recognized the broad, flat geological bag hanging from the seemingly shrunken shoulder. It was Regnar himself, the leader of the expedition that had been attacked in the crater. Radioactive readings indicated that the arctan had been hit with a blast from the Weyr; the counter revealed the characteristic presence of rare earth isotopes. Once again Rohan wished to take the geologist's ID tag, but this time he couldn't bring himself to. He merely unclipped the bag, because in this way he did not have to touch the body. It was filled with nothing but rock samples. After thinking for a moment, with his knife he prized off the monogram pinned on Regnar's leather jacket, slipped it into his pocket and, once again looking down from on top of a boulder at the motionless scene, tried to figure out what had actually happened here. It looked as if Regnar had fired at the robot, but had the robot attacked him or Bennigsen? In general, can someone suffering from amnesia defend themselves when attacked? He realized he would not solve the puzzle, and he still had more searching ahead of him. He glanced at his watch once again: It was coming up to five. If he had had only his own supply of oxygen, he would have had to turn back now. But it occurred to him to remove the oxygen tanks from Regnar's apparatus. He took the whole thing off the corpse's back, found one tank to be still full, and leaving his own empty one, he started to pile rocks around the remains. It took him the best part of an hour, but he felt the dead man had repaid him bountifully by sharing his oxygen supply. When the small mound was finished, it occurred to Rohan that it would have been good to arm himself with the Weyr, which was certainly still loaded. But again the idea had come to him too late, and he left with nothing.

It was almost six; he was so tired he could barely move his feet. He still had four energy tablets; he took one and after a minute stood back up, feeling a resurgence of strength. He didn't have the slightest notion of how to continue his search, so he walked straight ahead toward the rock gateway. He was about half a mile away when the counter warned him of increasing radioactive contamination. For the moment the reading was quite low, so he pushed on, keeping his eyes peeled. Since the ravine wound around, only some of the rock surfaces bore traces of melting; as he advanced, there was more and more of the characteristic cracked glaze, till finally he saw huge boulders entirely covered in frozen bubbles—their surface had boiled in the thermal impact. In fact there was no point continuing in that direction, but he kept walking. The counter on his wrist was now emitting a soft ticking sound that was ever faster, while the needle hopped like mad along the scale. Finally, in the distance he saw what was left of the gateway. It had collapsed into a hollow basin like a small pool of water that had frozen in some extraordinary way in mid-splash; the rock sediment had been transformed into a thick crust of lava, and the once black coat of metal undergrowth had become incinerated rags; in the background, amid the rock walls were hazy gaps of a brighter color. Rohan spun on his heel.

And once again chance came to his aid, as he was approaching the next rock gateway from the battlefield, this one much larger. Near a place he had already passed, the flash of a metal object caught his eye. It was the aluminum regulator from a breathing apparatus. In a narrow crevice between the cliff face and the dried stream bed was someone's dark back in a scorched jump suit. The corpse was headless. Some horrible blast had thrown it against some protruding boulders and crushed it. Nearby lay an undamaged holster containing a somewhat battered Weyr that shone as if it had just been polished. Rohan took it. He tried to identify the body, but it was impossible. He continued up the ravine; the light on its eastern slope was turning red and, like a burning curtain, was rising higher and higher as the sun dropped over the crest of the mountains. It was nearly a quarter of seven. Rohan was faced with a true dilemma. Up till now he had been fortunate, at least in the sense that he had carried out his task, he had survived, and could return to base. By his reckoning, the death of the fourth man was a foregone conclusion; in fact it had been thought extremely likely even back on the *Invincible*. He had come here in order to obtain certainty. Did he have the right to go back, then? Thanks to

Regnar's tank, he had oxygen enough for six more hours. Yet he had a whole night before him in which he could do nothing, if not because of the cloud, then simply due to the fact that he was close to utter exhaustion. He ate another energy tablet and, as he waited for it to kick in, he attempted to come up with a reasonably sensible plan for what to do next.

The black jungle high above him, along the edges of the cliff, was sunk in an ever more intense red glow from the sunset; individual spikes on the bushes glittered a deep purple.

Rohan still could not make up his mind. As he sat beneath the mass of broken metal, he heard the oppressive buzz of the cloud approaching from far off. Strange to relate, he felt no fear. His attitude toward it had undergone a remarkable transformation during a single day. He knew—or at least it seemed to him that he knew—what he was capable of, like a mountaineer uncowed by the death that lurks in the walls of glaciers. True, he himself did not fully understand the change that had taken place within him, for he could not recall the exact moment when for the first time, as the black bushes on the cliffs sparkled with every shade of purple, he had noticed their dismal beauty. But now, when he saw the black clouds—two of them were approaching, swarming from the slopes on the far side—he made no move, no longer sought shelter with his face pressed against a boulder. When all was said and done, his position made no difference so long as the concealed device was still working. With his fingertips he touched its coin-sized underside through the fabric of his suit and felt a soft vibration. He had no wish to court danger, and settled himself more comfortably so he wouldn't have to move. The clouds now covered both sides of the ravine; an organizing current seemed to pass through their black swirls, for they thickened at the edges, forming into almost vertical columns, while their inner parts bellied out toward one another and drew closer and closer. It was exactly as if some titanic sculptor were shaping them with extraordinarily rapid movements of his hands. A few brief flashes of lightning rent the air at the point where the two clouds were nearest each other; they appeared to be racing toward one another, yet each remained on its side, merely setting its central masses aflap in an ever fiercer rhythm. The glow from the discharges was oddly dim; both clouds were lit up for a split second—a billion silver-black crystals frozen in motion. Then—when the cliffs had repeated the peals of thunder several times over in a muffled echo, as if they had been covered with a fabric that stifled sound, the two sides of the black ocean joined together and interpenetrated one another, quivering in infinite tension. The air beneath them darkened as if the sun had set; at the same time bizarre, rapidly moving lines appeared in them, and it was only after a while that Rohan realized these were grotesquely distorted reflections of the rocky floor of the ravine. In the meantime, these airborne mirrors on the underside of the cloud undulated and stretched, till all at once he spotted an immense human figure, the top of its head extending into the darkness, that was gazing at him without moving, though the image itself trembled and danced without cease, as if it were continually being extinguished and then relit in a mysterious rhythm. And again several seconds went by before he recognized his own reflection floating in the empty space between the dangling sides of the cloud. He was so stunned, so paralyzed by the cloud's inconceivable action that he forgot about everything else. The thought flashed through his mind that perhaps the cloud knew about him, about the microscopic presence of the last living human amid the boulders scattered across the ravine, but this thought too failed to frighten him, and not because it was too fanciful—he no longer thought anything was impossible—but because he simply wished to participate in this ever more shadowy mystery, whose meaning—of this he was certain—he would never comprehend. His vast reflection—through which he could just make out the distant rocks of the cliffs in the upper part of the valley beyond the shadow of the cloud—was beginning to dissolve. Meanwhile, innumerable offshoots extended from the cloud; when it drew some of them back into itself, others took their place. From them, a black rain began to fall ever more densely. Some of the tiny crystals landed on him; they struck him lightly on the head, slid down his suit and gathered in its folds; the black rain kept falling, while the voice of the cloud, that roar filling not only the whole valley but the entire atmosphere of the planet, intensified. Local whirlwinds appeared, windows through which the sky could be glimpsed; the black shroud was torn apart in the middle and glided ponderously in a double bank, as if reluctantly, toward the bushes, till it descended into their stillness and vanished. Rohan continued to sit without moving. He did not know if it was all right to brush off the crystals covering him. They lay strewn across the boulders; the stream bed, which before had been bone-white, now looked as if it were spattered with ink. He took one of the triangular crystals gingerly between his fingers; it came to life, as it were, blew a gentle puff of warmth on his palm, and rose into the air when Rohan instinctively opened his hand. Then, as if at a sign everything around sprang into motion. Only at first was it chaotic. Then the black specks formed into something that resembled a layer of ground smoke; they gathered together and rose in columns into the air. It looked as if the rocks themselves were smoking from vast sacrificial torches that had no flame and gave no light. But it was only now that something truly unfathomable occurred: For when the rising swarm came to a halt in an almost perfectly spherical mass over the exact center of the valley, against the background of the gradually darkening sky, looking like a massive downy balloon of blackness, all at once the other clouds reemerged from the undergrowth and hurtled toward it at breakneck speed. Rohan thought he heard a bizarre grinding noise from the midair collision, but it was probably an illusion. He felt he was watching a battle, that the other clouds had expelled the inanimate insects from their midst and cast them to the bottom of the ravine in an effort to get rid of them; but the conflict was only illusory. The clouds parted and there was no trace of the sphere. They had absorbed it into themselves. A moment later, and only the peaks of the cliffs were bleeding in the last light of the sun, while the broad interior of the valley lay quiet and empty. Rohan rose on unstable legs. He suddenly seemed ridiculous to himself, with the Weyr cannon he had snatched from the dead man; more, he felt unnecessary in this landscape of perfect death, where only inanimate forms could survive and carry out their inscrutable actions that no living eye would ever see. It was not with horror but with stunned admiration that he had taken part in what happened a moment before. He knew that none of the scientists would be capable of sharing his feelings, but now he wished to go back not only as a messenger bearing news of the destruction of the missing men, but also as a person who would demand that the planet be left alone. Not everything everywhere is for us, he thought as he walked slowly downhill. By the light from the sky he was soon able to reach the battlefield. Here he had to quicken his pace, because the radiation from the glazed rocks, whose nightmarish outlines loomed in the gathering dusk, was ever more intense. In the end he broke into a run; the sound of his steps was repeated by some of the stone walls and reflected onto others, and in this perpetual echo that magnified his haste, leaping from rock to rock in a last burst of strength he passed the wreckage of the transporters, melted beyond recognition, and reached the winding slope, but even here the dial of the counter glowed ruby red.

He could not stop, though he was gasping, and so barely slowing down, he turned the valve on the oxygen tanks to the max. Even if the oxygen was to run out at the entrance to the ravine, breathing the air of the planet was decidedly better than staying here, where every inch of rock gave off lethal radiation. Oxygen throbbed coldly in his mouth. Running was easy, because the frozen river of lava the retreating Cyclops had left in its wake was smooth, in places almost like glass. Luckily his boots had a sturdy grip, so he did not slip. Now it had grown so dark that only the lighter colored rocks glinting from under their glaze showed the way downhill. He knew he had at least two miles to go on this part of the journey. Racing at full tilt as he was, there was no way for him to make any calculations, but still from time to time he glanced at the pulsing red dial. He could be here for another hour or so, amid the twisted and crumbling destruction of the rocks—that way the dose would not exceed two hundred Roentgens. An hour and a quarter even. If he failed to reach the desert by then, there would be no point in hurrying anymore.

Around the twentieth minute there came a moment of crisis. His heart felt like a cruel overpowering presence pushing outward, crushing his chest from inside; the oxygen burned his throat with a living fire, and sparks danced before his eyes.

Worst of all, he began to limp. Admittedly the radiation was decreasing, the counter fading in the dark like a dying ember; but he knew he still had to run, run on and on, yet his legs would not obey him. Every fiber of his body was spent, everything in him was crying out to stop, stand, or even collapse on the seemingly cool and harmless slabs of rock with their cracked glaze. When he tried to look upward, toward the stars, he stumbled and fell forward onto outspread arms. He sobbed as he gasped for breath. He stirred, got up, ran a few more yards staggering from side to side; then his rhythm came back and it swept him along. He had lost all sense of time. How did he orient himself in that soundless blackness? He had forgotten all about the dead he had found, about Bennigsen's skeletal smile, about Regnar at rest under his rocks beside the shattered arctan, about the headless man he had been unable to identify; he even forgot about the cloud. He was hunched over against the dark, which was filled with the blood of his eyes that were searching in vain for the great starry sky of the desert, whose sandstrewn emptiness seemed like salvation to him; he ran blindly, his eyelids bathed in salty perspiration, borne along by a strength whose unceasing presence within him he could still marvel at from time to time. This running, this night seemed to have no end.

He saw virtually nothing at all, when suddenly his feet found it harder to move, were sinking; he felt a final onrush of despair, raised his head, and realized he was in the desert. He could see the stars over the horizon; then, when his legs gave way beneath him, he looked for the dial of the counter, but could not see it: It was dark, silent, having left invisible death behind it, in the depths of the frozen channel of lava; that was his last thought, because when he felt the cool roughness of the sand against his cheek, he fell not into sleep, but into a trance in which his body was still laboring desperately, his ribs were working, his heart was thumping, but through the murk of utter fatigue he entered another, deeper darkness till he lost consciousness.

He woke with a jerk, not knowing where he was. He moved his hands, felt the cold sand trickling between his fingers; he sat up and gave an involuntary moan. He felt short of breath. He came to his senses. The phosphorescent needle of the pressure gauge showed zero. The other tank still contained eighteen atmospheres. He switched the valve over and stood up. It was one o'clock in the morning. The stars were etched against the black sky. He found the right direction on the compass and walked straight ahead. At three he ate his last energy tablet. Just before four his oxygen ran out. He jettisoned the apparatus and walked on, at first breathing cautiously, but when the cold air of early dawn filled his lungs he began to stride more briskly, trying not to think of anything except his march through the dunes, where from time to time he sank in up to his knees. He was a little like a drunken man, though he didn't know if it was brought on by the gases of the atmosphere, or if it was simply from weariness. He calculated that if he covered two and a half miles an hour, he would reach the ship at eleven in the morning.

He tried to check his speed on the pedometer, but he couldn't figure it out. The vast whitish trail of the Milky Way divided the dome of the sky into two uneven parts. He had grown sufficiently used to the wan light from the stars that he was able to skirt the larger dunes. He kept pushing on till against the horizon he saw an angular shape like a strangely regular gap among the stars. Not yet realizing what it was, he headed in that direction; he began to run, sinking in more and more deeply, but without even feeling it, till with outstretched hands, like a blind man, he felt hard metal. It was a jeep, empty, unmanned, perhaps one of those Horpach had sent out early the previous morning, perhaps another abandoned by Regnar's team. He didn't think about it, he simply stood up, breathing heavily, embracing the flat hood of the vehicle with both arms. Lassitude pulled him down toward the ground. To slip down by the jeep, fall asleep next to it, then set off in the morning once the sun was up ...

He slowly pulled himself onto the armor plating, groped for the handle of the hatch, opened it. The control lights came on. He slid into the seat. Yes, now he knew for sure he was disoriented, probably from the toxic effects of the gas, because he couldn't find the ignition, he didn't remember where it was, he didn't know anything ... Eventually his hand located the worn button of its own accord; he pushed it, the engine coughed softly and started up. He opened the cover of the gyrocompass; he only knew one number for sure, that of the return route. For some time the jeep rumbled along in the dark, Rohan having forgotten there were such things as headlights.

At five it was still dark. Then he saw, directly ahead of him, far away, amid white and pale blue stars, one ruby-colored star hanging low over the horizon. He blinked dully. A red star? There was no such thing ... He had the impression that someone was sitting next to him, probably Jarg, he wanted to ask him what star that could be, then suddenly he came to with a jolt as if he'd been struck. It was the bow light of the cruiser. He drove straight toward the red dot in the blackness. It rose gradually till it became a bright glistening sphere whose reflection glinted in the outer plating of the ship. A red light came on amid all the dials, and a buzzing sound warned of the presence of a force field nearby. Rohan turned off the engine. The vehicle rolled down the slope of the dune and came to a standstill. He was not sure he'd be able to climb back into the jeep if he got out of it. So he reached into a compartment, took out a flare pistol, and since his hand was shaking, he braced his arm against the steering wheel, held his wrist with his other hand, and pulled the trigger. An orange streak shot into the darkness. Its short trajectory burst apart all of a sudden as it struck the wall of the force field like an invisible sheet of glass. He fired over and over, till the pin gave a dry click. He was out of flares. But he had been noticed. The men on watch on the bridge had probably been the first to raise the alarm, as almost at the same time two large searchlights had been switched on near the top of the ship and, licking across the sand with their white tongues, had intersected at the jeep. At the same time, the ramp lights came on and the entire shaft of the personnel elevator lit up like a cold flame with a series of small lamps. In a split second the hatches were swarming with figures that came running, and mobile floodlights were turned on along the dunes by the stern, sending out swaying columns of light as they moved, till eventually two rows of blue lights indicated an opening in the perimeter.

The flare pistol had fallen from Rohan's hand. He didn't even know when he had slipped down the side of the vehicle; with unsteady, excessively long strides, unnaturally erect, his fists clenched to suppress the unbearable trembling of his fingers, he was walking directly toward the twenty-story high ship, which stood in a deluge of light against the pallid sky, so majestic in its unmoving bulk that it truly seemed invincible.

Zakopane, June 1962–June 1963